* * * * * * * * * *

Casey shrugged. "I've wanted to be an Elite gymnast for so long. Now that the time is here, I'm having a lot of doubts."

"Nothing's for sure, Casey. A lot of it is up here." Chip tapped his head. "Gymnastics can be a big mind game. Once you have the skills necessary for a particular level, it's up to you. But one thing is sure. You'll never make it if you don't believe in yourself."

"I have—until recently," Casey admitted.

Chip got up and walked around the desk. Casey stood up and he pulled her into a big bear hug. "You've got the stuff to do it, Casey. You've just got to want it badly enough."

Casey buried her face in Chip's T-shirt. She really didn't want to start with a new coach. Chip had brought her this far. Suddenly she realized how important it must be for him to have an Elite gymnast come out of his gym.

She pulled away and smiled at him. "If you'll help me, we'll do it together."

* * * * * * * * * *

Dream Time

PERFECT 10
4

HOLLY SIMPSON

FAWCETT GIRLS ONLY • NEW YORK

RLI: $\dfrac{\text{VL 6 \& up}}{\text{IL 7 \& up}}$

A Fawcett Girls Only Book
Published by Ballantine Books
Copyright © 1989 by Cloverdale Press Inc.

Library of Congress Catalog Card Number: 89-91313

ISBN 0-449-14592-1

Manufactured in the United States of America

First Edition: November 1989

To
My mother,
Mearle Hamblin

Chapter 1

★★★★★★★★★

CASEY Benson didn't know if she was jealous or not.

She stood in the loft at the Flyaway Gym Club, looking down at the uneven parallel bars, where her coach, Chip Martin, was checking out a new girl who wanted to be on the Class I gymnastics team. The girl was good—there was no doubt about that. And they did need another member on their team, since Casey's friend Jo Mallory had gone to California to study under the famous coach Boris Krensky. But Casey still felt uneasy as she watched Chip and the new girl stop and laugh.

She shook off the strange feeling. It was probably nothing. But she decided she'd work harder than ever to make sure she remained the best gymnast here at Flyaway. She and Chip had a special working relationship, and she didn't want anyone or anything to spoil it.

With the high school season over, Casey and her best friend, Monica Wright, had returned to Flyaway, a private gymnastics club where they trained the rest of the year. They needed a strong team as they headed into their Class I season.

I guess I'd better go down there and meet her, Casey thought. She ran her hands through her short curly hair, fluffing it up, and then checked her appearance in the mirror. Clear blue eyes stared back at her and she smiled, once again admiring her straight teeth. It had only been two months since her braces had been removed. Digging into her book bag, she found a tube of lip gloss and quickly applied some pink color.

On her way downstairs, Casey looked around the large, well-lit gym where she spent a good part of her life. Pale blue walls displayed murals of gymnasts swinging around the uneven parallel bars, going over the vault, or caught in movements from floor exercise. Her glance lingering on the figure of a girl poised on the balance beam, Casey smiled. When her father had owned the club, he had told Casey that she would look like that when she grew up. It had been five years since he'd sold the club to Chip, but she still considered that part of the mural to be hers.

"Casey!" Chip motioned her to come over to the bars. "I want you to meet someone."

Casey crossed the royal blue mats that covered the gym floor and stopped by Chip. On the top bar, the new girl paused, supporting herself with her arms.

"Casey, this is Sarabeth Walker." Chip adjusted his Chicago Cubs baseball cap. "She'll be part of our Class I team."

"Hi, Sarabeth!" Casey said cheerfully.

"Hi, Casey!" Sarabeth swung to the low bar and jumped down. "Chip says you're pretty good."

Casey glanced at Chip, who winked. "Thanks," she muttered to both of them. She studied her new team member, who was about the same height as she was—five feet one inch tall. Sarabeth's dark auburn hair, in a pixie cut, framed a round face with mischievous green eyes. A faint sprinkling of freckles spread across her nose. "Do you go to Fairfield High?" Casey asked.

"I'll be a sophomore—tomorrow." Sarabeth rolled her eyes. "My parents got me signed up here at the gym before the movers had even unpacked. They're very big on gymnastics."

"Aren't you?" Casey asked, surprised at Sarabeth's comment.

"Oh, sure. But I probably could have waited a day longer." She sighed. "You don't know what it's like having parents so stoked about gymnastics."

Casey smiled, thinking about her dad. He had been coaching for as long as she could remember, and even had been an alternate at the Pan American Games.

Chip coughed and again winked at Casey. "Oh, I think Casey knows."

"My dad is the high school coach," Casey explained.

"Oh, my gosh!" Sarabeth's eyes widened. "Were you on the team? Didn't you just flip out?"

"Let's just say it was a little rocky at times." Casey shuddered, thinking of the high school season and what a terrible time she'd had when her dad came down harder on her than any of her

teammates. But that was over now. She and her
dad had worked things out, and they'd finished the
season on friendly terms.

"Chip says you're going to try for Elite status at
the meet in March." Sarabeth let out a long whistle. "I'm impressed!"

"I'm working on it," Casey said, trying not to
look embarrassed. "How about you?"

"Not me! I'm content to compete on Chip's
team." She flashed Chip a big smile.

Tipping back his head, Chip laughed. "Flattery
will get you nowhere. Casey's an expert on that."

Just then, Monica Wright came out of the locker
room door with the rest of the team. Chip quickly
introduced the girls to Sarabeth and then told them
to start their warm-up exercises.

Casey pulled Monica aside, and they began
stretching together. "I got a letter from Jo," she
told her friend.

"Ooh, how is she?" Monica squealed. She wore
a hot-pink leotard, and her dark brown skin
glowed. Her hair was tied back with a narrow ribbon that matched her outfit. Monica was several
inches taller than Casey, and she had the slender
figure of a dancer.

"I saved it, like we promised," Casey said. She
and Monica had agreed to open the letters from
their friend together. No matter who received
them, they were always written to both girls. Before Jo had gone to California, they had been an
inseparable threesome—at school and at the gym.
Casey missed Jo terribly.

"So, where's the letter?" Monica demanded.

"It's in my book bag," Casey said. "We can read it after workout."

"Great!" Effortlessly, Monica stretched into her side splits. Leaning forward, she put her face on the mat.

Casey did the same thing, but couldn't help wincing. "How can you do these pancakes so easy? No matter how often I practice, I still can feel a few muscles."

"It's the long legs." Monica pushed herself up and sat cross-legged. "You're just too little." She dodged a friendly push from Casey.

Casey laughed. Monica had started gymnastics late, after many years of ballet training. But it had been love at first sight. After one class, Monica had decided to remain at the Flyaway Gym Club. She caught on quickly and soon was competing on the Class II team. Only last month, she had been moved up to Class I with Casey.

"Everybody over to the vault!" Chip called as the girls finished their warm-up exercises.

Casey noticed with satisfaction that the other three teammates were the same ones she'd competed with last year. Holly, with her long red hair in one braid down her back; Tracy, who was even taller than Monica and had more energy than the whole team; and Shannon, the petite blonde, the tiniest of them all.

"Let's warm up with half on, half offs," Chip said, indicating the compulsory vault they'd all have to do in their upcoming competition season. "Casey, you start!"

Casey focused her attention on the vault eighty-two feet down the runway. She started out running slow and picked up speed as she neared the spring-board Chip had set at the proper distance for her. The run was an important part of the vault, and Casey timed it right, punching the board with both feet and twisting her body halfway before her hands hit the vault. Pushing off, she rotated once again and landed solidly on the opposite side.

Chip threw his fist in the air. "All right!"

"I'm stuck!" Casey said, grinning. She didn't move her feet out of position. "You must have super glue on the mat!"

"You'll need super glue to stick your Yur-chenko!" Chip said, referring to the difficult op-tional vault Casey had started to learn. He reached for Casey, but she danced away at the last minute.

She giggled. "No way! These are Elite feet."

"Well, I hope you keep them for the Elite Trials," Chip said. He looked down the runway to the next girl.

Casey hoped she could continue sticking her vaults, too. For ten years she had trained in gym-nastics, first with her dad and then with Chip—all for a chance to go Elite and have a place on one of the national teams. Now she was getting close. After all those years, now it was only a matter of weeks until the Trials.

A couple of steps back, Chip stood watching. All the girls knew this vault so well, they didn't need much of a spotter. Still, Casey knew Chip was alert to any sign that one of them was in trouble, and would step up quickly to prevent that person from taking a tumble.

When Sarabeth came to the runway, Chip stepped forward, but she waved him back. "I can handle this one!" she called to him.

Sarabeth tore down the runway and sailed over the vault, getting a lot of height in her after flight. She landed perfectly, a good distance away from the vault. But on her way back to the line, she looked very nonchalant, as if her performance had been just so-so.

"Good job!" Casey said, smiling at Sarabeth.

Sarabeth shrugged. "It was okay. Nothing special."

After an hour, Chip motioned for them to stop and walked across the mats to the spring floor. "Let's stick with compulsories today and move over to floor ex."

While he dug through the tape case to find the compulsory music that was mixed in with each girl's original orchestration for her optional routines, the team began warming up on the floor. They took turns practicing the three tumbling runs that were part of each routine. These runs gave them the opportunity to show off their skills— power tumbling, Chip called it.

Floor exercise was Monica's best event, by far. All her years of dance training contributed to a graceful yet flashy routine. Even though she sometimes struggled with the uneven bars and the balance beam, no one could dispute she was tops on the floor.

"Go, Monica!" Casey yelled as her friend took her starting position. The others sat down along the mat to watch and wait for their own turns.

No matter how many times Casey had seen Monica perform, she was still mesmerized by the easy, flowing movements her friend made. It was as if Monica was one with the music. When she finished, the team gave her their usual round of applause. All of them wished they could do as well.

Workout flew by as Casey concentrated on her own routines but also kept her eye on Sarabeth. She told herself she was just sizing up the competition.

After completing their strength exercises, Casey and Monica raced upstairs to the loft to read the letter from Jo.

"Oh, I can't wait!" Monica bounced up and down as Casey rummaged in her book bag for the letter.

Finally, Casey found it and ripped open the envelope. "By this time, she should be able to tell us more about working with Boris. She really didn't say much in her last letter."

Monica laughed. "When she wrote that one, she'd only been there two days."

"I know, but I miss her so much."

"Well, so do I. Go on, read it!" Monica urged.

Casey sat down on a wooden bench and began to read the letter:

Dear Casey and Monica—my best friends ever,

Right away, I want to answer your question. No, I haven't found any good friends yet—and none that will ever replace the two of you. Everyone is so competitive here. Each girl is going to try for a spot on the Olympic team, and no one gets that friendly with the competition. I miss the spirit we had at Flyaway, but mostly I miss you.

"Doesn't she say anything about Boris?" Monica asked.

"Hold on, there's more." Casey turned to the second sheet and continued to read:

Boris is certainly a maniac for work. Even your dad can't hold a candle to him, Casey. He does motivate everyone. He makes you want that Olympic gold so bad, it hurts. But I'm so afraid I'll make a mistake. One day, I fell off the beam twice, and everyone just stared at me. No one told me it was okay—because to them it wasn't. I could have used a hug from you guys that day—every day, in fact.

Anyway, I'm toughing it out, and who knows, maybe Boris will actually make an Olympic gymnast out of me.

Love you tons,
Jo

Neither Monica nor Casey said anything for a minute. Casey felt a twinge of remorse. She had wanted to be chosen by Boris so badly that even though she was happy Jo had been selected, she couldn't help feeling hurt.

And what if Jo went to the Olympic Games without her? Since they'd been ten years old, they'd planned to make it together. Now it looked as though Jo might leave her behind.

Monica frowned. "Do you think she sounds happy?"

Casey shook her head. "No, but maybe working with Boris is enough. Maybe you're not supposed to be happy, too."

"Well, I don't know," Monica said softly. "But I think I'm glad to be right here. Only I wish Jo was with us."

A tear rolled down Casey's cheek. "I know. I miss her a lot, but she wanted this so much. At least she has a chance to reach her goal."

Monica gave Casey a hug. "You're going to make it, too. And you'll do it representing the Flyaway Gym Club."

"We'll all make it. We still have over two years until the next Olympics." Casey smiled weakly. She wished she could believe what she just said.

Chapter 2

★★★★★★★★★★★

THE next morning Casey burst into the art room. First period ranked as her favorite class, in spite of her lousy art work. This was all due to a certain blond boy with blue-gray eyes with whom she shared an art table—and an occasional movie.

Casey jerked to a stop. She couldn't believe her eyes. Her new teammate, Sarabeth, was sitting in *her* spot, next to Brett Kelly. Sarabeth flashed her brilliant smile up at Brett, who stood leaning back on his elbows against the window ledge. Neither of them had seen Casey come into the room.

What is she doing in my place? Casey thought as she watched them. *And why does she have to be in* my *art class?* Casey wanted to run up and hang a Taken sign around Brett's neck. But she couldn't do that, and it wasn't exactly true. She and Brett hadn't agreed to "go together," but they did attend a few school activities and games with each other. Casey stifled a giggle. She wondered if she could get Brett to sign a formal contract. She

11

sighed. Actually, with gymnastics, she didn't have the time. And anyway, he seemed to be enjoying Sarabeth's company, more than she would have liked.

Brett looked up and saw Casey standing by the door. "Well, are your feet set in cement or what?" he teased her. He smiled a warm welcome as Casey walked over.

"Hi, Brett. Hi, Sarabeth." Casey placed her book on the table directly in front of the other girl.

Sarabeth gave her a friendly grin. "Hi, Casey! I registered this morning. I'm so glad you're in this class."

Casey noticed that Sarabeth looked at Brett as she said that, and again a twinge of jealousy shot through her. *Stop it*, she told herself. *Sarabeth is new and she's just trying to make some friends.*

"You two know each other?" Brett asked.

"Sarabeth joined the team at Flyaway Gym yesterday," Casey said.

Suddenly, the smile left Sarabeth's face. "Yeah, I just *had* to fill up every minute of my time," she said.

Surprised at the sarcasm in Sarabeth's voice, Casey wondered if she wanted to be at Flyaway at all. She guessed it would be hard to leave a gym and move clear across the country—to get used to a different coach and make all new friends. She wouldn't want to do that, either. She knew how hard it had been for Jo.

"Casey sits here," Brett told Sarabeth. "I think there's an open table over there." He pointed to an empty chair next to a redheaded boy who painted a lot of watercolors.

Sarabeth looked back at the place Brett had indicated and shrugged. "I can take a hint."

"What made you decide to take art?" Casey asked. "Do you draw or paint?"

Sarabeth got up from the table. "Neither. I'm terrible at art. But this was the only elective open!"

"The same thing happened to me." Casey told her about having to switch out of sixth period journalism so that she could get to practice early. "This is definitely my worst subject," she told Sarabeth. "and I mean *worst*."

Sarabeth's eyes lit up. "You mean, you're not as good an artist as you are a gymnast?"

Brett laughed. "You mean Michelangelo, here?" He dropped his arm across Casey's shoulders. "She's trying to be a sculptor."

"He means, he's showing me how to shove a chunk of clay into a recognizable project," Casey said. She liked having Brett's arm around her.

"Well, anytime you want to help me, I'll be right over there." Sarabeth winked at Brett as she gathered up her purse and spiral pad and headed for the empty chair.

Casey watched her walk away, noticing how easily she struck up a conversation with her new table partner. She shook her head. It wouldn't take Sarabeth long to blend into the school and get rid of the "new girl" label.

"Will you have breakfast with me?" Brett reached into his pocket and pulled out a crumpled napkin.

"You know I don't eat Snickers bars for breakfast," Casey said.

"Aha! But there's a new menu!" Brett whipped out a package of two granola bars from his pocket. "See how big an influence you've been on me?"

"Just because my dad's a nutrition freak doesn't mean *I* like all that stuff." Casey took one of the bars and sat down. "If I wasn't a gymnast, I'd probably eat lots of garbage."

"Garbage! I'm offended." Brett perched on the edge of the table. He gingerly tasted the granola. "This better be good for me."

"Don't worry, it is," Casey said. "Why are you here so early?"

"I had a meeting for Winter Carnival." Brett jumped off the table and took a bow. "Ta-dah! You are looking at the chairperson of the sophomore snow sculpture."

Laughing, Casey congratulated him. "That's fantastic! It'll be a work of art, I'm sure."

Brett grinned at her. "We'll be in competition with you lowly freshmen. Have you had an organizational meeting yet?"

Casey shrugged. "With gymnastics, I never have time for this kind of stuff. But it does sound like fun."

"Winter Carnival is a great weekend—there's the snow sculpture competition, ice skating, the basketball classic, and"—he rubbed his hands together—"the class princesses."

"And I bet *that* is your favorite part," Casey observed.

"We-e-ll," he drawled, "unless someone I know

would come out and help me do some snow sculpting. You have to be better at that than you are with clay," he teased her.

"Hey, we're competitors. I can't help you," Casey observed.

Brett grimaced. "Couldn't you take a lot more classes and get sophomore status in a month?"

"Oh, sure! I'll notify the counseling office today!"

Just as Mr. Green, the art teacher, walked into the room, Casey broke into a fit of giggles. Mr. Green gave them a questioning look, and Casey put her hand over her mouth to stifle her laughter.

Glancing back over her shoulder, she saw Sarabeth watching her and Brett. When their eyes met, Sarabeth gave Casey a little wave and smiled.

For the rest of the period, Casey looked through some art magazines, trying to decide what her next project should be. She'd spent a million hours working on a clay dolphin, and if it hadn't been for Brett, she'd have never got a passing grade.

Brett raced through his art projects with his own jet-plane speed, each one looking great. Today he'd started kneading and getting the air out of a piece of white porcelain clay.

When the bell rang, Casey and Brett walked out of the room together. Sarabeth came out right behind them.

As Casey said good-bye and left for history class, she heard Brett say to Sarabeth, "Hey, you're a sophomore! Why don't you sign up to work on our Winter Carnival snow sculpture?"

Casey wasn't sure she liked the idea of Sarabeth

working with Brett. She seemed to really like him, and it was obvious that she could put the charm on guys when she wanted to.

What if Brett ended up falling for Sarabeth?

Chapter 3

"I couldn't believe the way Sarabeth flirted with
Brett," Casey told Monica as they dressed for
workout at the gym that afternoon.

Monica pulled up her leotard. "Of all the nerve!
She's here one day, and she thinks she can take
over!"

"She's a good gymnast, and I guess she'll be good
for the team," Casey said reluctantly, throwing her
duffel bag into the locker. "But I don't like the way
she looks at Brett."

"We won't let her get away with that," Monica
assured her.

Snapping the combination lock shut, Casey hesitated. "Well, don't come on too strong. We still
have to work with her."

"Don't worry. You know me better than that."

Casey laughed. "That's exactly why I *am* worried."

Monica finished dressing and looked down at her
blistered hands. "I don't think I'm going to be

working bars much today. I really ripped yesterday."

Casey examined Monica's palms. "You've been practicing hard lately."

Monica shrugged, shut her locker, and grabbed her small towel. "C'mon, let's go. You know how Chip gets if we're late."

In the gym, the rest of the team had already started their warmups—everyone except Sarabeth. Casey peeked into Chip's office and up at the loft. Sarabeth had definitely not arrived.

The gym was strangely quiet that afternoon, with only the Class I team. When school let out and all the beginning gymnasts came for lessons, it could get really loud. As long as she could remember, Casey had been excused from last period gym class to go directly to the Flyaway Gym Club.

"Where's your buddy?" Monica interrupted Casey's thoughts as she began stretching her legs.

Casey shrugged. "Chip is going to flip out! Her second day, and she's late." She reached her arms over her head, twisting to give her body a good stretch.

"Have you seen Sarabeth?" Shannon asked. She was stretching on the mat next to Casey. "Chip's starting to look at the clock." Weighing only eighty-five pounds, Shannon hardly looked old enough to be in the eighth grade.

Shaking her head, Casey said, "She checked into school today, but I haven't seen her since lunchtime. She was eating with the cheerleaders."

"I think she's going to get in trouble," Shannon predicted.

After they'd finished warming up, Chip called the team over to the uneven parallel bars area. They all piled down on the crash pad, a mattress-thick cushion that absorbed their landings.

Once again, Chip glanced at the clock. "Does anyone know anything about our newest team member?" He looked around at the girls, who shook their heads. "Listen up! You know how I feel about promptness. I give you plenty of time to get here after fifth period—don't I?"

Hesitantly, Casey decided to speak up for Sarabeth. "This is the day they moved into their house. Maybe she had to help unpack."

Chip frowned. "When they registered, her parents assured me she'd be here every day. Anyway, let's get on with practice. I'll deal with her when I see her."

Monica looked questioningly at Casey. "Why are you putting in a good word for Sarabeth? I thought you didn't like her," she whispered.

"I like her okay . . . I just don't want her flirting with Brett." Casey pulled her knees up to her chest and wrapped her arms around them. "Anyway, I think she'll add to our team. Without Jo, we need her to win the Zone Championship this year."

Monica nodded. "That's for sure!"

"Ladies, if you're finished?" Chip glowered at the two friends. "I'm splitting you into groups. I want you to work on optionals today. Spot each other and spend about half an hour on each event. The Class IIs will have the vault first. And remember to look out for the little ones when they get here."

Casey and Monica paired up, as usual, and

walked over to the balance beam. "You go first.
You're the one that loves this brutal event," Monica said.

"I just try to forget it's only four inches wide,"
Casey said as she hopped up on the beam.

"Yeah, right," Monica said as she stood by to
spot Casey.

From across the gym, Chip yelled, "Save the new
combination until I get over there!"

Casey nodded and waved at Chip. Then she
grinned at Monica. "I've been working on this
combination since last August, and he still calls it
new." Casey had been working on a difficult back
handspring layout for the end of her routine. She
had done the stunt in a tuck position for a long
time, but now she wanted the extra difficulty that
came with the layout. She hoped to make it a per-
manent part of her routine for the Class I season
and for the Elite Trials in March. She'd need it in
order to make the top level of gymnastic competition.

"I can see it now. The newsman is interviewing
Chip after you've won the Olympic gold medal."
Monica held up a fake microphone. "Chip nods and
says, 'If there had been a problem it would have
been with the new combination. Once she got
through that, she was home free.' "

"And when they interview me, I'll say I owe my
gold medal to the new combination," Casey said,
throwing her hand to her forehead in a dramatic
gesture.

"This is not a comedy club!" Chip hollered.

Choking back her laughter, Casey began warming up. To get the feel of the beam, she did a few kicks and turns and ran through her routine without the difficult elements. Finally, when she felt at ease on the beam, she began practicing each of her harder moves. When she had finished, she let Monica warm up.

Monica took her turn loosening up and slid into the splits, stretching her head to her knee.

"Try your handstand from there." Casey moved in to spot her friend.

"Agh! You know I hate those," Monica said, shifting into front splits before she lifted herself off the beam, balancing on her hands. Slowly she began pushing herself into the handstand position. Halfway, her elbows started buckling, and Casey stepped forward to steady her.

"Okay, now take it up." Casey supported her friend until she had her balance.

When Monica jumped down, she shook her head. "I'll be ancient before I get those. I can see it, a twenty-year-old gymnast still working on handstands!"

"You just need more arm strength," Chip said as he came up to the beam. "And you know what *that* means."

Both girls groaned. Arm strength meant one thing to Chip—handstand push-ups!

"Let's try it again." Moving closer to the beam, Chip waited to spot Monica.

Monica hopped onto the beam and slid effortlessly into her splits, facing Chip. Once again, when she reached the halfway point, she started to waver.

"Easy . . . just shift your weight a tiny bit forward. . . . That's better," Chip coached.

On the corner of the crash pad, Casey sat watching Chip patiently help her friend. That was one of the reasons her dad had selected Chip to buy the Flyaway Gym Club when he decided to go back to teaching at the high school. But as patient as Chip seemed now, she knew he could instantly change if one of his gymnasts didn't follow his rules or started goofing off . . . as Sarabeth already had.

Glancing around, Casey saw that she still hadn't arrived. Now she was almost an hour late.

The gym was coming alive with young beginning gymnasts chattering together as they gathered for class. The Class IIs had also arrived and were assembling at the vault area with one of the assistant coaches. She waved at Jill Ramsey, who had recently joined the Flyaway Gym Club. After becoming friends with Casey while they competed together on the high school team, Jill had started going with Casey's brother, Tom.

Chip interrupted her thoughts. "Okay, Benson, get up there. Let's work on the new combination."

Casey climbed onto the beam and positioned herself to go into a back handspring.

"Just do the flip first," Chip said as he adjusted his cap.

Casey did several single handsprings and then two in a row. Finally, Chip told her to try the layout combination.

With her back to the beam, she stood at the end, preparing herself mentally. She concentrated hard, thinking only of the difficult maneuver.

"Spring high. Stretch out!" Casey heard Chip's voice as she threw her body backward into the air. After completing the handspring, she launched into an aerial back somersault, stretched out in layout position.

She landed, wobbled slightly, but managed to stay on. From her perch on the low beam, Monica applauded.

"Atta girl!" Chip gave her a thumbs-up sign. "Let's try a few more while I'm here."

"Can I use it in the first meet?" Casey asked, hopeful he'd finally give it his okay.

Chip thought a minute, then nodded. "I've been thinking about letting you put it in. Now that we have six people on the team—*if* we have Sarabeth—we can afford to gamble on it." Only five scores counted in the Class I meets, so if Casey's combination didn't work, her score would simply be thrown out.

"Thanks, Chip, you're the greatest!"

"Get back to work!" Chip scowled, but he couldn't quite cover his smile, and Casey knew he wasn't mad. "You, too!" he barked at Monica, who jumped to her feet and went back to work on the low beam.

After Casey had tried six more combinations, Chip left to help Shannon on the uneven bars. On four of the six attempts, Casey had stayed on the beam, and she almost saved the last by bending forward at the waist. Instead, she jumped down. In competition, the judges deducted nearly as much for a series of wobbles as they did for falling off the beam.

"Hey, look over there!" Monica pointed to Chip's office.

Whirling around, Casey saw Sarabeth come in from the locker room. "Uh-oh."

"I think it's time to move to the vault, don't you? The Class IIs are done." Monica nodded at the runway to the vault, which started near the office, where Chip stood talking to Sarabeth. "We've spent more than our half hour here anyway."

Casey smiled. "Great! Which one of us gets to spot down by the horse, and which one gets to eavesdrop?"

Laughing, Monica nodded toward the vault. "Holly's over there. Let's get her to help us. Then we can both listen in." They walked over to the end of the runway. "Hey, Holly! Will you spot us?"

Holly nodded. "Where does your board go?" she called from the horse, ready to adjust the springboard.

While Holly got the board ready, Casey and Monica listened to Chip as he lit into Sarabeth.

"Where have you been? You're over an hour late!" Chip was practically shouting. Monica and Casey could have heard him from clear across the gym.

"I just got out of school," Sarabeth said meekly.

"At three o'clock?" Chip demanded. Holly walked over to join Monica and Casey.

Sarabeth looked away and pulled at her leotard, which was printed with soft pastels that faded one into another. "I came right after sixth period."

"Don't you have P.E. sixth period? What about

your last school? Didn't you get excused early there?" Chip asked.

Shrugging, Sarabeth kept looking at the mat. "Well, I . . . yes, but I didn't know if it was the same here."

Chip threw up his hands. "Well, *ask* next time!"

As Sarabeth started to move away, Chip continued, "And if you want to be on this team, don't be late again! If you end up in the hospital or need an appendectomy, call and ask permission first!"

Without looking at the team that had gathered a few feet away, Sarabeth headed for the mats to warm up.

Turning around, Chip saw the rest of the team watching. "What do you think this is—an exhibition? Get back to work!"

Quickly, they spread out and resumed practicing.

When Sarabeth finished warming up, she joined Monica and Casey at the vault. "Wow! Does he ever get mad!"

Casey nodded. "He's a real stickler for being on time."

"So I noticed! Do *you* come every day at two o'clock?" Sarabeth asked.

Surprised at her question, Casey turned to look at the new girl. "Of course! What did you do, stay for sixth period?"

"Yes, I did," Sarabeth said. But for some reason, Casey suspected that she hadn't gone to her last class.

"What's with you?" Casey asked. "I'm sure Chip

told you yesterday that you were supposed to be here at two. Don't you want to be on the team?"

"Sure, but I hate to have to rush here every afternoon," Sarabeth argued.

"Well, those are the rules." Casey shook her head.

"If I had a book, it might not be so boring down here!" Monica yelled from her position down by the vault.

"Sorry!" Casey ran down the runway and popped over the horse in a handspring vault to warm up.

"What's Her Majesty have to say?" Monica asked.

Casey shrugged. "Not much. She stayed for sixth period—I guess."

Monica raised an eyebrow. "Do you think she really did?"

"Who knows! Go on, I'll spot both of you—if she wants to work out at all."

Ready to vault, Sarabeth waved to Casey, who left the springboard at her own setting, since they were the same height.

Sarabeth pounded down the runway and exploded over the horse doing a half on, half off. She left the springboard and twisted before her hands hit the horse, and then again as she sailed off the other side. Once again, Casey was impressed with her power. "Great vault!" she congratulated Sarabeth. "That's a terrific leotard."

"It's okay." Sarabeth ran her hands over the colorful leotard that clung to her petite form. "My mom made it. She's into all these fabric dyes."

"I love it! Does she ever sell them?" Casey asked.

"No way! She doesn't want *anyone* to look like her precious daughter," Sarabeth said, rolling her eyes in apparent disgust.

Casey detected a problem between Sarabeth and her mother. She thought about her own family. She was glad they were supportive and basically easygoing—at least now that she'd ironed out the problems she'd had with her dad.

Casey waved for Monica to start. "Okay, Monica! Go for it!"

The girls took turns spotting each other as they worked up to their own optional vaults. When their time was up, they moved on to bars. Sarabeth left them and wandered over to the beam.

After she'd gone, Monica turned to Casey. "What do you think of her?"

"I really don't know." Casey shook her head. "But I think there's something going on we don't know about. I hope it doesn't hurt the team."

Chapter 4

★ ★ ★ ★ ★ ★ ★ ★ ★

AFTER workout Thursday night, Casey waited for her brother, Tom, to pick her up in his car. Since basketball practice ended about the same time, he swung by to get her. A few months ago, she wouldn't have believed that she and Tom could actually be friends.

Casey hopped into his restored Chevy Camaro, and Tom pulled away from the gym. "I heard you have a new girl on the team," he said.

"Word travels fast." Casey couldn't believe how quickly news got around at Fairfield High.

"You don't sound overjoyed," Tom said, glancing at her.

"I don't know. She's fun, and she's a good gymnast . . . really explosive on the vault, but . . ." Casey's voice trailed off.

"Are you sure you're not just a little bit jealous?" he teased.

"Probably," Casey smiled. She knew that not so long ago she would have reacted to his comment by turning away, refusing to speak to him, and probably slamming the car door when they got home. But recently they had learned to get along— they even liked each other.

"Hey, what's this? Casey Benson actually agreeing with her big brother?" Tom grinned.

"Amazing, isn't it? But something seems wrong about the whole thing with Sarabeth. She's always late to practice, and half the time she doesn't even act like she wants to be there," Casey said.

Tom chuckled. "Maybe I should get to know her."

"Forget it! You've already got Jill." Casey shook her head. Her good-looking brother attracted most of the girls at school. Besides having a muscular build and wavy dark hair that always fell in his eyes, he was the star receiver on the Fairfield High football team. When Casey had arrived at the school last fall, all the senior girls had tried to be friends—just so they could meet her brother.

"Jill *is* pretty special," Tom agreed.

"She sure is! She took you out of circulation!"

Casey's thoughts returned to the gym. "Anyway, this stuff about Sarabeth may be nothing. Just my overactive imagination."

After pulling into the Benson driveway, Tom parked off to the side. He got out to shove a large piece of cardboard under the car to catch the oil drips, while Casey headed for the house.

During the high school season, Casey's mom often held dinner until they could all eat together. Now, back at Flyaway, practice lasted until eight, so Casey and Tom usually warmed up their food in the microwave oven.

In the hall, Casey dumped her books on the table and headed for the kitchen, where Mrs. Benson greeted her as she took the foil off a plate. "Hungry?"

Casey poured a glass of milk. "Starved! Tom'll be down after he showers."

"How was practice?" Mrs. Benson pushed back her short, soft brown hair. Like Casey, she had a petite frame, though she stood an inch taller than her daughter.

"Good. Chip said I could do my layout in one of the meets soon."

After pouring herself a cup of coffee, Mrs. Benson brought Casey's dinner and sat down with her. "It's about time."

"Now that we have six girls on the team, he can chance letting me try it."

"Who's taking a chance on what?" Bear Benson walked into the room and rumpled her hair.

Tipping her head back, Casey smiled at her father. His dark curly hair had recently acquired a generous sprinkling of gray. He worked out to keep in good shape, and as he leaned over Casey to give her a hug, she could feel the muscles in his arms. "We're talking about Sarabeth Walker. She's just come to the gym."

"Chip mentioned he was getting a new girl." Mr. Benson went over to the coffeepot. "So, how is she?"

Casey decided not to share her concerns about Sarabeth. As close as her dad was to Chip, word would certainly get back to the gym, and she wasn't ready to mention any doubts she had to her coach. "She's a great vaulter. And pretty flashy on the unevens. She'll never replace Jo, though." Casey sighed, thinking about her friend, before she continued. "But since we can't have Jo back, Sarabeth will be a good addition to the team."

"It's a good thing she came along right now," Bear commented.

"I know," Casey said.

She only wished she felt that way about Sarabeth and Brett.

On her way to art class the next Monday morning, Casey wondered if she would find Sarabeth in her seat again, talking to Brett. Entering the room, she saw Sarabeth was already there—only this time she was discussing something ,with Mr. Green. Casey shook her head. It was strange that Sarabeth could always be on time for art but never for workout.

For a second or two, she watched Brett, his blond curly head bent over his clay. Just looking at him made her pulse start off on a sprint.

A few feet from the table, Casey stopped again to study the new piece of sculpture he was molding in milky-white porcelain clay. She frowned. To her, it looked like a Life Saver standing on its side.

"I see you've started a great . . . oh, I know—a tire!"

Stepping back to look at the piece, Brett grinned. "I'm glad you like it. It's a whitewall."

"Of course. I should have recognized it immediately," she joked.

Brett tipped back his head and gave a hearty
laugh. Then he dropped into his chair and grinned.
"How was your weekend?"

*It would have been better if I could have talked
to you,* Casey thought to herself. "It was okay."

"No gymnastics?"

"Only Saturday morning. I just hung out with
Monica the rest of the time," Casey said.

"I got a weekend job at Hippo's Burgers," Brett
volunteered, then added hastily, "Working days."

"I'm glad it's not at night," Casey said, a little
too quickly, and then felt herself begin to blush.
She hoped he wouldn't think she had plans for his
free weekends. She smiled. Actually, she had lots
of ideas on how he could fill them.

Brett grinned. "Me, too! I told them I couldn't
work the weekend of Winter Carnival."

Casey waited for Brett to ask her to go with him,
but he kept talking about his job.

"I'm saving for a car. My uncle's got a hot Mus-
tang he'll sell me as soon as I get the money," Brett
explained.

Disappointed that he didn't invite her to at least
one part of the carnival, Casey tried to be enthusiastic about his future car. "That sounds good,"
she said.

"Good? It's fantastic! We'll have a great time!"
Realizing that he was including her, Brett red-
dened and quickly looked away. He grabbed a
sponge and began to wet down the clay again.

From her side of the table, Casey could see a smile creep onto Brett's face, and she felt a warm glow. She would love to be part of his plans. She pictured the two of them riding together in Brett's car along the shore of Lake Michigan. It would be spring, and the breeze would blow through her hair. . . . Brett would put his arm around her. . . .

Then reality cut her daydreams short. Now that he had a job and her Class I competition season started this weekend, there wouldn't be any time for them to spend together. She sighed. At least, Sarabeth would be busy with gymnastics, too.

"We keep the supplies in the cupboard," Brett teased.

Casey laughed. Brett knew he had caught her daydreaming. "I was just visualizing my project." She raised an eyebrow. "Isn't that what you told me to do?"

"You'll never *have* a project if you don't get busy."

Casey pulled out her clay and carving tools. Mr. Green had suggested she try a second clay piece of a group of dolphins so she could show them together in the student art show in May. She looked down at her piece. So far, the school of dolphins looked like a can of limp sardines with bulging eyes staring back at her. "I think I need more help," she said to Brett.

He reached over and guided her hands, showing her how to smooth out the lines.

At that moment, Casey didn't care if the dolphins looked like jellyfish. She just hoped he couldn't hear her heart beating louder than a bass drum.

Casey met Monica for lunch in the cafeteria. They carried their trays to their favorite table by the windows. As she slid into her chair, Casey noticed large posters advertising the Winter Carnival tacked on the walls. "This must be a big deal," she said, nodding at the signs.

Monica nodded. "Yeah, they're having a huge ice skating party at Fletcher's Park."

"Did Derek ask you to go with him?"

"Not exactly. But he sort of hinted at it," Monica said.

"Well, he will." Casey broke her hamburger in half and took a bite. When she looked up, she saw Jill Ramsey, her brother's girlfriend, coming toward them.

"Hi, Casey, Monica." Jill set a box on the table and opened it. "Do you want to buy a Winter Carnival button? The senior class is selling them. It's to help cover expenses for the skating party and the snow sculpture."

Casey picked out one of the red-and-white buttons that showed a comical snowman urging them to support the carnival.

"Is the carnival as much fun as everyone says?" Monica asked.

"It's the most fun thing this winter. And if we win the basketball classic again this year, it'll be great." She smiled at Casey. "Tom's already asked me to go skating and to the game."

Casey groaned. She could just see it. Everyone would have a date and she'd have to go alone. And she didn't have Jo to go with, either.

"What's this game?" Monica asked.

Jill sat down next to them. "It's the final game of the week-long winter tournament."

The girls continued to talk about the carnival until Jill remembered she had to get back to selling buttons. Before she moved to the next table, Casey and Monica had each bought a button.

As Jill left, Casey pinned her button on her pocket. She sighed and looked out the window. "I hope I get to go with Brett."

"Who else would he ask?" Monica eyed her friend. "Don't even suggest it. He's *not* going to invite Sarabeth."

Casey hoped Monica was right.

"With the dual meet tomorrow, we should have a shorter workout today," Monica observed as she and Casey headed toward the Flyaway locker room on Friday afternoon.

"Usually, he lets us out early the day before. Look, he's smiling. That's a good sign," Casey said.

As they opened the door to the locker room, they heard a cheer echoing off the tiled walls.

"Rock 'em! Sock 'em! Fairfield High! We're going to leave them high and dry!"

Casey exchanged glances with Monica, who shrugged as they watched Sarabeth doing a cheer on the bench. In her hands, she waved blue-and-gold pompoms that belonged to the cheering squad at school.

"Rah, rah! She's on time!" Casey whispered.

Monica stifled a giggle. "Where did she ever get that cheer?" she whispered back.

Sarabeth jumped off the bench in a split leap. As she landed, she whirled around and saw the girls standing there.

Sarabeth didn't seem a bit embarrassed to have been discovered jumping around. She waved the pompoms over her head and said, "Yeah, Fairfield."

Casey gave Sarabeth a thumbs-up. "Not bad."

Monica headed for her locker. "You're really getting into your new school."

"I'm just practicing. One of the cheerleaders loaned me her pompoms." Sarabeth sat down next to Casey, who had tossed her gym bag on the bench and started to open her lock. "Have you ever been a cheerleader?" Sarabeth asked.

"No way," Casey answered as she pulled out a navy-blue-and-white-striped leotard. "I've been in gymnastics since I was five."

Sarabeth's eyes widened. "That's practically your whole life. No wonder you're so good!"

Casey felt herself begin to blush. "You should see our best friend, Jo," she said. "She's gone to California to study with Boris Krensky. She's great!"

Monica walked over as she tied her hair back with a ribbon. "Don't let her kid you, Sarabeth. Casey's just as good as Jo."

"How long have you been in gymnastics?" Casey asked.

Sarabeth rolled her eyes. "It seems like forever. Actually, since sixth grade. My parents signed me up. They thought it would teach me discipline. Agh! Do I ever hate that word!"

"Don't you want to be here?" Casey asked, frowning.

Sarabeth looked at Casey's concerned face and then at Monica. "Lighten up! Of course, I want to be here. Who wouldn't want to work with Chip?"

"We need you on the team," Casey said, relieved to hear Sarabeth liked their coach.

Jumping to her feet, Sarabeth shook the pompoms again. "I just wish there were time to do cheerleading, too!"

The door banged, and Holly and Shannon came in to dress. Monica looked at the clock. "Speaking of time, since you're here, why don't you surprise Chip and be ready to start with the rest of us?"

Sarabeth laughed. "I guess I could use a few Brownie points." She opened her locker and quickly started to pull off her jeans.

"C'mon." Casey poked Monica. "Let's go warm up."

"Oh, wait for me, please." Sarabeth gave Casey a pleading look. "I'll hurry."

Glancing quickly at the clock, Casey saw they still had five minutes. "Okay, but dress fast."

When she was ready, Sarabeth thanked them for waiting, and they went into the gym together. As they walked over to the mats to stretch out, Chip looked at the threesome and raised an eyebrow. "Glad you could join us so early, Sarabeth," he said.

Sarabeth just gave him a little wave before she started her warm-up exercises.

"I'd have melted into the mat if he said that to me," Casey whispered to Monica.

Monica nodded and concentrated on stretching out her long legs. "Nothing seems to bother her."

After warmup, the girls ran through both their compulsory and optional routines a few times, in preparation for the dual meet against the Evanston Eagles the next day. Sarabeth stayed with Monica and Casey during each rotation. As the afternoon went on, Casey couldn't help enjoying Sarabeth's company and laughing at her jokes.

At four o'clock, Chip called everyone together. "I wish I could say our first meet would be our easiest," he began. "Most of our duals will be just optionals, but this meet will show how we compete with the compulsories, too. And the Eagles team is good. They think they can beat us."

"We'll show them!" Shannon, the smallest team member, shouted.

Chip grinned. "That's the right attitude! Now, go home and get a good night's sleep. No partying!" He paused, and then looked directly at Sarabeth. "And I would appreciate all of you being on time in the morning."

He dismissed them, and after they'd changed, Sarabeth said good-bye and caught the bus home. Since they were early, Casey and Monica walked.

Even at four-thirty, the gray skies had started to darken, and the sky promised more snow before morning. Casey shivered in the cold afternoon air.

Stuffing her gloved hands in her pockets, Monica said, "I don't know what to make of Sarabeth."

"Me, either." Casey started to slide on the icy sidewalk, but caught herself. "But tomorrow we'll see just how good she is in competition."

Monica nodded. "I hope it's good enough."

Chapter 5

★★★★★★★★★★

SATURDAY morning, Casey finished her warmups and pulled on her sweats, to wait for the start of the meet. She could see her mom and dad sitting on the bleachers Chip had assembled after they'd left the night before. Parents and younger brothers and sisters made up most of the audience. It seemed strange not to have a lot of high school kids talking and laughing, ready to cheer them on.

Shaking her head, she realized that even though the level of gymnastics was much higher at the Class I meets, in some ways they didn't seem as exciting as the high school meets.

Monica finished her warmups and came over to join Casey.

"It's not quite as exciting without the noisy crowd," Casey said.

"I know. That cheering really psyched us up," Monica agreed.

Casey remembered Monica and Jo's success at drumming up a big group of students to come to one of the high school meets, and they'd kept coming back. Casey smiled as she thought of the matching shirts Brett had silk-screened for his friends in the cheering section, and a large helium-filled balloon with her name on it that he always brought to the meets.

"It'll be easier to concentrate, I guess," Casey added. She didn't mention how much she wished Brett could be there. With his new weekend job, he'd never make any of the meets.

"Over here, Flyaways!" Chip called them together to give them the order in which they would perform. Since the scores tended to build with each gymnast, the last girl was expected to score the highest. Because Sarabeth's scoring ability was still unknown, Chip had her lead off on beam and floor. On bars, he placed her in the middle, where she was excellent some days and fell off others.

"I think Chip's placed her exactly right," Casey whispered to Monica.

"Even though she goes after you on vault?" Monica asked.

"Chip knows what he's doing," Casey said.

The team nodded its approval when Chip announced Monica would be last on the floor, where she excelled, and Casey would anchor the beam and bars.

Dropping her arm across Monica's shoulders, Casey gave her friend a squeeze. "I'm so excited! We're going to do it!"

"We sure are!" Monica squeezed Casey's arm. "I see a win in our future."

From the first notes of music, when the teams

marched in to take their positions, until the compulsory part of the meet was over, the two teams concentrated on the exact skills required of each girl. Throughout the meet, the compulsory music repeated over and over as each gymnast went through her routine. This first day, it was important to be technically correct but still add special individual flair. The next day, each girl would compete with her own optionals routine.

When the points were added, the Flyaways were ahead of the Eagles. Crossing her fingers, Casey hoped they could hold on to their lead.

The next morning Casey stepped out of the shower and went to her closet. A large poster of Mary Lou Retton covered the door. Since the 1984 Olympic Games, Mary Lou had been Casey's idol. She also had a poster of 1988 Olympian Phoebe Mills on her wall.

Casey reached into her top dresser drawer and pulled out the leotard she wore for optionals. She loved the shiny red-and-navy-print Lycra fabric. She quickly dressed and then inspected herself in the mirror.

In the hall, the phone she shared with Tom rang loudly, breaking the silence. On a Sunday morning, Tom wouldn't be up until late. Casey hurried and picked up the receiver on the second ring.

"Hello, may I speak to Casey?" a boy asked. Casey instantly recognized Brett's voice, and her heart began to pound.

"Hi, Brett! What gets you up so early?"

"How'd you know it was me?" he asked.

Casey laughed. "I've heard you talk before, remember?"

He paused. "Not on the phone."

"Well, maybe we should try it more often,"
Casey said.

"Good idea! Anyway, I'm on my way to work, and
I thought I'd call and wish you good luck today."

A warm glow spread through Casey. He had remembered. "Thanks. We're ahead at this point, but
optionals are today."

"You'll kill 'em!" Brett said enthusiastically.
"How's Sarabeth doing?"

Casey's heart sank. Why did he want to know
about Sarabeth? Trying to be honest, she said,
"She's done a great job. Her compulsories were
right on."

"Well, I'm sure she's not as good as you are,"
Brett told her. "Gotta go! The business world calls!"

Casey smiled as she hung up the phone. She
wasn't happy that Brett had asked about Sarabeth,
but at least he was still *her* number-one fan.

Downstairs, she ate breakfast with her father before they left for the gym. Her mother wouldn't be
at the meet because she had gone to the University
of Illinois to watch Casey's older sister, Barbara
play a tennis tournament. Usually, Mrs. Benson at-
tended all of Casey's meets. She'd been a physical
education teacher before Casey was born, and she
loved sports.

Bear Benson would be judging one of the events
that day. He often helped Chip. At first, Casey had
been nervous when her dad judged her, but she
soon found he was extremely fair. She didn't re-

ceive any bonus points, but he didn't mark her
lower than the others, either. She guessed they had
both learned a lot from working together on the
high school gymnastics team.

Casey quickly finished her bowl of cereal. Putting on her team sweats, which were navy with
red stripes on the legs and sleeves, she fingered
the small Flyaway emblem near the collar.

Bear put his arm around Casey as they headed
for the garage. "How many sets of Flyaway sweats
do you think you've gone through?" he asked.

"Too many to count!" Casey answered, grinning.

On the short drive to the gym, Casey considered
the optional part of the meet. The Evanston Eagles
weren't far behind, so everyone on her team would
have to do well today in order to win. Still, if they
kept going the way they had yesterday, she
thought the Flyaways would come out on top.

After warmups, Casey stood waiting to march in.
She still felt anxious about the day ahead. Looking
into the bleachers, she was surprised to see three
boys from Fairfield High sitting at the top, leaning
back against the wall. She wondered whom they
had come to watch.

When the music started, the team walked in, led
by a young Class III gymnast who carried the Flyaway banner. They lined up in the center of the
mats with the Eagles, and each girl stepped forward when Chip introduced her.

"Look," Sarabeth whispered to Casey. She nodded toward the boys Casey had noticed earlier.
"They're in my English class."

Trust Sarabeth to have rounded up an audience, Casey thought.

The Flyaways started the meet on the vault. Relieved not to have drawn the balance beam first, Casey relaxed. She liked having the vault first because it gave her a chance to shake out her nervousness before the other events.

"What vault are you doing?" Sarabeth asked. Once again, she was seeded to be the last girl on this rotation, so she would follow Casey.

"I'm doing my Tsukahara today," Casey answered, visualizing the vault in her mind. She'd do a half twist onto the horse and then push off into a front somersault.

"Me, too." Again, Sarabeth looked up into the bleachers. She gave the boys a little wave. Turning back, she said, "I thought you had Yurchenko."

"I do, but you're not supposed to compete with it if you're not an Elite." Casey watched Holly complete her vault. "I'm hoping Chip will let me do it at the American Classic."

When it was Casey's turn, she saluted the judges and focused on the horse at the end of the runway. Punching the springboard, she sailed over the vault. Satisfied, she grinned at Chip, who gave her a little pat as she returned for her second attempt.

Sarabeth, the Flyaways' last vaulter, was expected to score the highest. This was her best event, and Casey watched hopefully as Sarabeth stood poised to begin. As she saluted the judges, she smiled into the bleachers.

Casey gasped, astonished at Sarabeth's lack of

concentration. How could their newest teammate be thinking of guys at such an important moment?

In spite of her lack of attention, Sarabeth's vault had tremendous afterflight and she landed solidly. The audience applauded loudly, and the three boys gave her a standing ovation. A well-dressed couple jumped to their feet, and the man shook his hands over his head. Casey figured they were Sarabeth's parents.

Sarabeth beamed and stepped out to acknowledge the crowd's enthusiasm. Casey noticed that she turned away from her mom and dad.

As they moved to floor exercise, Monica asked, "What's going on with her?"

Frowning, Casey sat down in the second-position chair next to Monica. "Sarabeth's got a cheering section in the top row." She knew she sounded disgusted, but she didn't try to hide it from her best friend.

"Well, a 9.3 is not too shabby." Monica leaned back in her chair. "It'll give us a good lead."

Casey agreed. "I know, and we may need it later."

Shannon started the floor exercise rotation. Designed to accent her small size, her routine was full of cute, quick movements, and her orchestra music was fast and lively.

Sarabeth got up earlier than usual to stretch out and practice her turns behind the row of chairs. She whirled and held each one in a pose.

"Look at Miss Showoff," Monica said as they both watched Sarabeth.

Casey rolled her eyes. Then, shaking her head, she turned back to watch Holly.

A few minutes later, Sarabeth began her floor exercise, which had been choreographed at her last gym to her own choice of wild, crashing music. The unusually stirring routine had exciting movements, but Casey thought Sarabeth was adding new dramatic touches as she went along. She continued to glance into the audience as she danced her way across the mat.

"What's with her?" Monica whispered.

Casey knew gymnasts who were experts in playing to the judges in floor exercise, but Sarabeth seemed more interested in the three guys in the bleachers. "It's like she's performing just for them," she said.

Chip stood on the sidelines, his face set in a deep scowl. Casey knew there would be fireworks when Sarabeth finished.

Monica nudged Casey. "Here's her last tumbling run."

As Sarabeth ran diagonally across the spring floor, she threw herself into a roundoff, back handspring, and then into a double back in the corner of the mat. When she landed and punched into a forward front somersault, she had too much momentum and took several steps to avoid falling. She ended with an exaggerated pose, which she held a moment too long.

Chip rubbed his forehead and stared at Sarabeth. He looked as though he couldn't believe what he'd just seen.

When Sarabeth's score was flashed—a 7.8—her smile faded. So did Casey's.

"That'll kill us!" she said to Monica.

Monica gestured toward the side of the gym, where Chip was obviously lecturing Sarabeth. "Speaking of someone who's going to get killed . . ." she observed.

"He should have talked to her *before* the meet," Casey said, letting out a long breath. "It may be too late now to do any good."

Even Monica's spectacular floor routine and Casey's performance on the beam couldn't bring back the lead they'd had before Sarabeth's fiasco. When they went to the uneven bars, they were tied with the Eagles.

"If only Jo were here," Casey moaned.

"If she were here, she'd win it for us on bars," Monica agreed.

Turning in her chair so she could keep an eye on the Eagles, Casey said, "I wonder how good they are on the beam?"

"I don't know, but we can't depend on them to make a mistake," Monica argued. "We'll have to score well ourselves."

Casey laughed. "You sound like Chip—but you're right." She leaned back and sighed. "If only we could depend on Sarabeth. Sometimes she can be great on bars."

"Chip had a long talk with her after floor exercise. She looked pretty unhappy during beam." Monica took off her sweat jacket as Tracy started on the bars.

"That's just what we don't need—Sarabeth unhappy. We need more from her than an average routine," Casey said.

Sarabeth walked over, and Monica slid down to make room between her and Casey. Seeded second to last, Sarabeth had to do well on bars to set up the scoring for Casey. She took her seat without saying anything. She looked dejected.

When it was closer to Sarabeth's turn, Casey tried to cheer her up. "Go for it, Sarabeth! You can make a difference!"

Sarabeth smiled weakly. "I'll try."

Casey wondered how all this affected Sarabeth. Was she really sorry she'd put the team in jeopardy? Chip must have come down hard on her. At least, she'd stopped flirting with the boys.

In front of the bars, Monica saluted the judges and began her routine. Casey was sure Monica couldn't help them pull ahead. This was her worst event, and her palms were still ripped from workouts. Even the long hours of practice hadn't produced the results her friend had tried so hard for. Casey didn't understand it.

She caught her breath. Monica almost didn't get her legs up in time and barely missed hitting her foot on the low bar when she came out of a high bar handstand and shot over. Sarabeth grabbed Casey's arm as they watched Monica finish with no steps.

Relieved, Casey let out a long sigh. Monica had made it without a major deduction, but the score was still close. Now it would depend on her and Sarabeth.

Holly completed her routine, and Sarabeth

stepped on to the mat. Casey watched her square her shoulders and concentrate. To herself, Casey whispered, "Don't blow it."

Sarabeth was spectacular. She worked from the high to the low bar smoothly, and her dismount had the height the judges looked for in a good routine. Even before the 9.1 flashed, Casey could see the pleased look on her face.

With more difficult elements in her own routine, Casey scored a 9.3, and then they all sat down to wait for the Eagles to finish on the balance beam.

It seemed to take forever, but when the team's scores were finally announced, the Flyaways had won by a half point. Casey watched Chip shake hands with the Eagles' coach. His usual exuberance was missing. They had pulled it out, but he was not happy.

"Chip is going to have a lot to say on Monday," Monica told Casey as they changed in the locker room afterward. "Did you see his face?"

"That meet was too close," Casey agreed.

"Thanks to Sarabeth," Monica added as she tossed her leotard into her gym bag.

"Well, she did come through for us in the end. And she got second place on bars." Casey scanned the locker room for Sarabeth, but she wasn't there.

Monica frowned. "I don't see how she can be a klutz one minute and a champ the next. That bar routine was terrific! She hardly works at all, and look at her routine." Monica glanced at her own torn-up hands and shook her head.

Casey gave her friend a hug. "One of these days,

everything will click, and you'll be fantastic on bars."

Monica pushed her away and laughed. "I wish I had your confidence."

"Well, I don't have much confidence in our winning the team competition at Zone unless we do something about Sarabeth."

Monica nodded in agreement. "Do you have any ideas?"

Shaking her head, Casey said, "Unfortunately, no. But we'll have to think of something. We can't have this happen again."

Even as she spoke, Casey wondered what they could possibly do with a free spirit like Sarabeth, who only seemed to care about the team part of the time. They'd never win the Zone Championship if she continued to let them down.

Chapter 6

★★★★★★★★★★★★

THE next morning, Casey was still trying to think of what they could do to make Sarabeth care about the team. So far, she'd drawn a blank.

In art class, she found Sarabeth sitting on one of the tables at the back of the room with two juniors on the boys' basketball team. Casey giggled. *Boys again!* Maybe if they stopped giving ribbons at gymnastic meets and gave away dates instead, Sarabeth's concentration would improve.

"What's wrong with you?" Brett asked as Casey sat down at their table. "Did you lose the meet?"

"No, we won—barely," Casey said.

"Did you have a bad day or something?"

Hesitating, Casey decided the problems at the gym were not something she should share, even with Brett. "Not really." She dumped her books on the table and decided to change the subject. "How was Hippo's?"

"Educational! I had to watch six videos on how to warm a cherry pie."

Casey groaned. "Sounds like a drag."

"How can you say that?" He dropped his chair down with a thud. "Next weekend I get promoted to French fries."

"Ooh," Casey pretended to swoon. "And are you getting more money for that?"

"No, just more grease."

They both laughed, and when Mr. Green came into the room, Brett picked up a drawing pad and began sketching Casey.

"Hey! What are you doing?" Casey looked around for Brett's circular sculpture. "Where's your tire?"

Brett hesitated. "I had a flat."

"What happened to it?"

A smile flickered at the corners of his mouth. "I must have picked up a nail. The man at the garage said it couldn't be fixed."

Casey shook her head. "What are you going to make now?"

"No more clay. I'm going to draw your portrait." He sketched a few more broad strokes.

"C'mon Brett, you're making me nervous."

"Smile! You don't want me to sketch a frown on your face, do you?"

Casey gave him a dirty look and went to get her supplies.

For the rest of the period, she tried to find out what had happened to Brett's sculpture, but he just grinned and continued sketching her. And when she tried to peek at his drawings, he whipped them out of her reach. Finally, she gave up. He obviously wasn't going to let her see them until he was ready.

When the bell rang, they walked out the door together. Sarabeth caught up to them in the hall. She smiled sweetly at Brett. "It looks like I'll be able to come tonight," she told him.

"Great!"

Casey stopped. Had Brett asked Sarabeth to go out? She didn't understand. He hadn't paid much attention to her in class. Maybe they saw each other somewhere else. No matter how many times Casey told herself Brett wasn't interested in Sarabeth, she still didn't believe it. If only she felt sure of his feelings for her! But they had never really talked about being anything more than friends to each other.

Sarabeth waved and headed for her next class, but Casey just stood in the hallway. She felt as though her feet were frozen in place.

Brett winked at Casey. "Too bad, freshman. Your snow sculpture won't stand a chance of winning at the carnival—especially now that we have Sarabeth working for us."

So that was it, Casey thought. They were just going to the sophomore committee meeting that day. She knew Brett was teasing, but she still felt uneasy about him and Sarabeth.

As she finished her strength exercises after practice, Casey once again found herself thinking about Sarabeth. If she wasn't worrying about Brett, then she was stewing about Sarabeth's effect on the team. Why couldn't she put that girl out of her mind?

The whole workout had been different than she'd expected. Anticipating a lecture from Chip, the team had found him strangely quiet. Occasionally he scowled at Sarabeth, but mostly he ignored her and let the team work on their own. He'd come over to Casey when she was on the beam and told her she'd done a good job in the meet. "We'll let you do your new combination next time," he added, to her delight.

Now, as the team finished for the day, the phone rang in Chip's office. Casey stopped when she heard him say, "No trouble, Donna. She's right here." He motioned to Casey. "It's your mom."

Surprised, Casey ran in and took the phone from Chip. "Hi, Mom! Is anything wrong?"

"No, I just wanted to catch you before you left the gym," Mrs. Benson said. "Jo left a message on the machine that she'd call you tonight at nine. She's hoping Monica can be here, too."

"Oh, Mom, that's terrific! I'll let her know. See you later!" She handed the receiver to Chip with a hurried "Jo's calling tonight" and raced to the locker room to find her friend. "Monica! You have to be at my house at nine. We're going to talk to Jo!"

"That's great!" Monica grabbed Casey into a hug and whirled her around.

"It'll be so good to hear from her," Casey said, wiggling out of Monica's exuberant embrace. "Will your mom let you come?"

"I'll be over right after I eat."

"Okay, see you." Casey grabbed her duffel bag

and spun in a pirouette before she danced out the door.

She could hardly eat her dinner, and when she finished, she ran to her room, taking the stairs two at a time. Opening her algebra book, she planned to do some homework before Monica arrived, but it was no use. She could not sit still.

The clock on the wall said eight-forty. She couldn't believe it. In twenty minutes, Jo would call. It would be so good to hear her voice. She hadn't thought she would miss her so much.

It had been hard when Boris Krensky had chosen Jo to study with him at his gymnastics school. Casey had been happy for her friend but, at the same time, disappointed that Boris hadn't wanted her, too. She had told Jo that it hadn't mattered to her, but whenever she thought about it, it still hurt.

The door slammed, and Monica raced up the stairs, out of breath. "I . . . I had to wait until my mom got home from the office."

"You made it!" Casey flipped her book shut. "Let's go wait by the phone."

The girls went into the hall. Casey sat cross-legged on the floor, and Monica slumped into the beanbag chair. The minutes dragged by, and the two girls stared at the phone, waiting for it to ring. Finally, when the call came at five after nine, both Casey and Monica lunged for it.

"Hurry, get on Tom's extension," Casey said as she picked up the receiver. "Jo! Is that you?"

"Casey? Monica? Are you both there?" Jo's voice came over the line.

"Jo! It's great to hear from you!" Monica exclaimed. "How good are you getting?"

"I bet you're ready to take on Julianne MacNamara," Casey said, referring to Jo's favorite gymnast, the American uneven bars medalist in the 1984 Olympics.

Jo giggled. "Yeah, right! You guys are great! I haven't laughed in weeks. Everyone's so uptight here."

"I bet they love you," Monica said.

"No way! Remember, I'm the new girl here." Jo sighed. "And anybody good is a threat."

Jo didn't sound like herself, Casey realized. Her usual optimism was missing. "But you're so lucky to be there," Casey encouraged her.

"I don't think so," Jo replied. "I wish I was home with you guys. I hate it here!"

"It can't be that bad!" Monica protested. She walked over to the door, pulling the long phone cord behind her, and gave Casey a questioning look.

Casey shrugged as Jo went on. "We're at the gym for six or seven hours a day. The girl I'm living with, Debbie Lancaster, is a terrific gymnast, but she skips out on practice and asks me to cover for her. Then her mother gets mad at *both* of us."

"C'mon, Jo. *You're* getting to study with Boris. And you're going to make it!" Suddenly, Casey wondered if she would make it, too. Staying at home and working at the Flyaway Gym Club didn't seem like the best road to the Olympics.

When they hung up fifteen minutes later, Casey sat on the floor staring at the phone until Monica came out of Tom's room. "That sure didn't sound like Jo," she said, shaking her head.

"She doesn't seem very happy, does she?" Monica asked.

"Here she is, studying with one of the greatest coaches, in an exciting gym . . . she'll probably have a good chance of making Elite, and—"

"She wishes she were back here." Monica finished Casey's sentence for her.

"I guess it's the old grass-is-greener bit. But I'd sure like to be there," Casey said. She imagined how it would feel if she were in California. She pictured herself flying over the vault and then looking up at Boris for advice.

"So would I, though he would never have chosen me." She studied Casey for a moment. "But Boris wasn't so smart when he overlooked you," she told her friend.

"Thanks, Monica. I did feel pretty rotten about it," Casey said, for the first time admitting to Monica just how badly Boris's decision to take only Jo had affected her.

Monica put her hand on Casey's arm. "I'm sorry. I know you must have felt terrible."

Monica stayed another hour, and they tried to tackle their homework together. Finally, they both decided it wasn't going to work. They were getting nowhere. How could either one of them concentrate on math when they were worried about Jo?

For the next several days, Casey thought about her real chance of making it as a national-level gymnast. She was fifteen and too old to be in the

Junior Elite program. Her dad had encouraged her to wait—to work hard with Chip and then to go for Elite status at the meet in March. But should she have accepted his advice? she wondered. Maybe if she had pushed him to let her study with a famous coach, she'd be in a better position to make a national team.

But maybe staying home and working with Chip was the right way for her to go for Elite. She just didn't know anymore!

By the end of the week, Casey knew she had to talk to someone about it, so she hurried to the gym club after school. If she was going to speak to Chip in private, she'd need time before the other team members arrived.

Slipping through the door, she found Chip working on the corner of the spring floor, where the carpet had come loose. She stood behind him and watched as he closed the can of contact cement and got to his feet.

"Oh, what's this? A spy?" Chip asked when he turned and saw her.

Casey shook her head. "Do you have a minute?"

When Chip noticed her solemn expression, his grin disappeared. He draped his arm across her shoulders. "I think this calls for an office visit," he said as they headed across the mats.

Casey didn't say anything until he had closed the door and she'd dropped into his large, comfortable old chair. "I needed to talk to someone," she said frankly.

"You've come to the right place." Chip tipped back in his swivel rocker and put his feet on the desk. "I sense this has something to do with gymnastics. You've been quiet all week."

"I should have known you'd notice." She picked at the loose upholstery on the arm of the chair. "Why didn't you say something?"

Chip shrugged. "I figured, when you were ready, you'd come in without my prodding."

Casey was glad she had come to see Chip. He had a way of making her feel better, no matter what was wrong. They had worked together for so many years that he knew her inside and out. Taking a deep breath, she blurted, "Do I have any chance at all of making Elite?"

"Of course you have a chance!" Chip swung his feet down off the desk and leaned forward. "Where'd you get the idea you didn't?"

Casey looked down. "Well, I talked to Jo Monday night and . . . well, she's out there working with all those super gymnasts."

"And you think that because you stayed at home, you don't have the same chance," Chip concluded.

"Yes, I guess so—no, I don't know. But Boris told Jo he'd make her an Olympic contender . . . and he does have a lot of gymnasts on national teams."

"And you're stuck here in Flyaway, with only Chip Martin to coach you." He slumped back in his chair.

"It's not you! I love working with you!" Casey hated herself when she saw the look on Chip's face. She hadn't meant to make him feel badly. All she'd wanted was some help with her own problems.

"But you think with Boris you'd have been a shoo-in?" Chip asked.

Casey shrugged. She felt worse now than when she'd come into his office. "I've wanted to be an Elite gymnast for so long. Now that the time is here, I'm having a lot of doubts."

"Nothing's for sure, Casey. A lot of it is up here." He tapped his head. "Gymnastics can be a big mind game. Once you have the skills necessary for a particular level, it's up to you. But one thing is sure. You'll never make it if you don't believe in yourself."

"I have—until recently," Casey admitted.

Chip got up and walked around the desk. Casey stood up and he pulled her into a big bear hug. "You've got the stuff to do it, Casey. You've just got to want it badly enough."

Casey buried her face in Chip's T-shirt. She really didn't want to start with a new coach. Chip had brought her this far. Suddenly she realized how important it must be for him to have an Elite gymnast come out of his gym.

She pulled away and smiled at him. "If you'll help me, we'll do it together."

"That's more like my girl." He lifted her chin and wiped away her tears with his thumb. "C'mon, I can't have my best gymnast all wet and soggy!"

Chapter 7

★ ★ ★ ★ ★ ★ ★ ★ ★ ★

SATURDAY afternoon, Casey sat on her bed looking out the window through the bare branches of the large maple tree that stood guarding her room. She was trying to decide if she should do something special for Valentine's Day. Her mom had offered to let her have a party like last year's, but she didn't know enough guys at the high school, and except for Monica, most of her girlfriends were from the Flyaway Gym Club and went to other schools. She wasn't sure what to do.

"I wish Jo were here!" she said aloud to Mary Lou Retton, who smiled down from the poster on the closet door. "It won't be the same without her."

She wondered if she would see Brett on Valentine's Day. She certainly hoped so. Should she buy him a valentine card? What if he didn't give her one?

She giggled. She could send him a telegram: "Very important announcement—please take note. Valentine's day arriving. Don't forget Casey

Benson!" Grinning, she pressed her nose to the frosty window and watched the snow falling outside. Brett would be happy about this, she thought. It looked as though it was the right kind of snow for making sculptures—heavy and wet.

"Casey!" Mrs. Benson called from the living room. "Monica's here!"

"Send her up!" Casey sat down on her bed and listened as her friend ran up the stairs.

Monica burst into the room. She'd left her coat downstairs, but snowflakes still clung to her hair and eyelashes. "I was so bored this afternoon. I should be doing that history reading, but . . ." She spread her hands in resignation.

"I know what you mean. I've been sitting here like a vegetable."

Monica giggled. "I don't think anything's sprouted yet," she teased as she joined Casey on the bed.

Casey noticed her friend's silly expression. "I don't suppose you came over for anything else—other than to avoid homework?" she asked.

"We-e-ll, I *did* get a phone call." Her face widened into a big grin.

"Tell me!" Casey squealed. "Did you hear from Jo again?"

"No." Monica flounced onto her stomach and gave Casey her most sophisticated look. "It was *not* from a girl."

"Derek called? Why didn't you tell me?" Casey demanded.

"I haven't had a chance!"

"Did he invite you to Winter Carnival?"

Monica's brown eyes glowed. "He asked me to the skating party . . . and we're going to the basketball game, too."

Hugging Monica, Casey bounced up and down on the bed. "That's terrific! When did he call? I just saw you at the meet this morning."

Monica was still grinning. "About ten minutes ago."

"You sure took a long time getting here," Casey said with a giggle.

"Well, I didn't want to rush too much. It was nothing special, you know." Monica tried to look nonchalant.

"Oh, Monica, I knew he'd ask you."

Monica squeezed Casey's arm. "Brett will ask you, too."

Instantly, Casey's enthusiasm died. "I don't know. All he talks about these days is his precious snow sculpture."

"There's still lots of time." Monica looked up at the gymnastic pictures on the walls. "You know, you'll have to make room for your own poster one of these days."

Casey looked at the posters. Her friend had hit on one of her dreams—having her own poster. She smiled, remembering the time she'd tried out poses in front of her mirror. Maybe someday it would come true.

"Hey, you were fantastic in the meet this morning!" Monica went on. "I think I held my breath during your entire beam routine."

Casey flopped back on her pillow. "I was so glad Chip let me do the layout."

"It's about time!" Monica agreed.

"I wanted to show him I could do it in competition," Casey said.

"Well, you sure did. It looked great. And we'd have needed your extra points if Sarabeth hadn't come through today," Monica pointed out.

Casey nodded in agreement. "We never know when she'll blow it. She's so inconsistent. It's frustrating."

The phone rang, and Casey's mom hollered up the stairs again. "Monica! It's your mom."

"Uh-oh. What now?" Monica went into the hall to get the phone. When she returned, she wore her coat—and a frown. "Gotta go, Casey. I left my history book open on my desk by mistake. Mom saw it and called to make sure I'd finished. I'll see you later, okay?"

"Bye. Thanks for coming over," Casey said.

After Monica left, she grabbed her white teddy bear and curled up on the bed. Her thoughts returned to the dual meet against Park Forest that morning. She'd worn the copper-enameled earrings Brett had given her for Christmas, and they'd brought her luck. She remembered the exhilaration she'd felt when she landed her layout combination with nothing more than a slight wobble. Chip's smile could have lit the whole Park Forest gym, and when she scored the 9.7, he'd hugged her until she hurt. She smiled to herself. She'd like to hurt like that more often!

Everyone had congratulated her—even members of the other team.

Sarabeth had linked elbows with her after the

meet and told her how impressive the layout combination had looked. "You're a celebrity now," Sarabeth had said. "And I'm so glad you're my friend."

Casey felt guilty for all the things she'd said and thought about Sarabeth in the past few weeks. But Sarabeth could be so exasperating with her hot-and-cold attitude toward the gym. There was no way Casey could begin to understand her.

Only when Chip asked her to come over to meet the Park Forest coach was Casey able to pry herself away from Sarabeth.

Chip draped his arm over her shoulders and introduced her to the opposing coach. "This is Casey Benson, Bear's daughter. She's my hope for the Elite Trials next month."

The coach shook Casey's hand. "If today's any indication, I'm sure you'll make it."

A gust of wind moaned against the window and brought Casey back to the present. She gave her teddy bear a hug and decided to go down to see what the rest of the family was doing. As she left the room, she glanced at her posters. "Move over, Mary Lou. I may be joining you soon."

Monday morning, Casey was still elated over the meet. She stopped at her locker before art class and saw Brett coming down the hall toward her. Brett waved and bowed deeply. "Good morning, Your Highness. I hear you're Queen of the Balance Beam."

She was surprised he knew about the meet, but she felt pleased. "Yeah, I did my layout yesterday."

"So I've heard. Sarabeth hasn't stopped talking since she got here!"

Casey looked around for her teammate. "Where is she? I haven't seen her this morning."

"I saw her outside with one of the cheerleaders. They took off together."

"I hope she remembers to come back for class. She gets a little goofy when she's with them," Casey observed.

"She's goofy most of the time!" Brett chuckled.

Casey watched his smile, wondering if he liked Sarabeth that way. She reached up and touched the earrings she still wore. "Your earrings brought me luck in the meet."

Brett frowned. "I thought you hated them. You always wear those gold ones."

Casey's eyes widened. "Silly, I had to get my ears pierced after you gave them to me. And you have to wear studs for at least six weeks before you can wear anything else."

Brett looked at her for a minute before he spoke. "You had your ears pierced so you could wear *my* earrings?"

When Casey nodded, he looked away and studied the row of lockers, but Casey could see a tiny smile flickering at the corners of his mouth.

Suddenly he blurted, "What are you doing on Valentine's Day?"

"I don't know yet." He must have gotten my mental telegram, Casey thought to herself.

He looked at Casey. "I—I was wondering . . . well, if you had a meet on Sunday?"

Casey noticed that the usually outgoing Brett

was having trouble speaking. Could he actually be nervous for once? "No, we're off," she told him.

"I was just wondering . . . if you'd like to do something?"

He's certainly doing a lot of wondering, Casey thought. "Sure, I'd like that," she said.

"You didn't have anything better planned?"

"Better than what?" Casey couldn't help teasing him.

Brett seemed to relax. "I thought we'd go on a picnic."

"A picnic!" Casey looked out the window at the snow drifting on the school lawn. "Are you serious?"

"Don't tell me you haven't been on a snow picnic before?" Brett said.

She shook her head. She couldn't believe he was actually asking her for a date. But she liked the idea of going off somewhere with him. She was always game to try something new—only this time, she wouldn't have a spotter to guide her. "Don't you work on Sundays?" she asked.

Quickly he began rearranging the books in his hands. "Uh, I already got it off," he muttered.

Casey smiled as they started off to art class, nearly bumping into Sarabeth, who flew in the door as the final bell rang.

"What's that smile on your face for?" Sarabeth asked as Casey greeted her.

"Oh, nothing," Casey said.

Chapter 8

★ ★ ★ ★ ★ ★ ★ ★ ★ ★

SUNDAY morning, Casey woke up early and looked out her bedroom window to check the weather. Valentine's Day had finally arrived. The frosty icicles hanging from the roof glistened in the bright sun, which reflected off the snow in the backyard. It looked as if it was going to be a perfect winter day. She giggled. Only Brett would have thought up a picnic this time of year!

As she climbed out of bed, she saw a square white envelope tucked under her door. She ripped it open and pulled out a valentine from her parents. Mrs. Benson was really into celebrations, and Casey knew that evening her mom would serve a special family dinner, as she did for each holiday. The rest of the family always teased her mom that they were the only people in Chicago who celebrated every holiday on the calendar—even Groundhog Day.

Going over to her desk, Casey pulled out the card she had bought for Brett. She and Monica had gone to the card shop together, and they'd spent over an hour reading all the valentines before they each decided on one.

Picking up her pen, she started to write her name on the valentine. She hesitated, unsure how she should sign it.

"Love, Casey," she said aloud. She couldn't say that! But then she couldn't say, "*Like*, Casey," either.

She looked into the mirror and laughed. "Hugs and kisses, darling," she said to her reflection in her most dramatic voice, as she pictured herself in a flowery, ruffled dressing gown, signing the card with a large, romantic scrawl.

Collapsing in a fit of giggles, she decided "Your friend, Casey," would be just fine.

She wiped her eyes as a knock sounded on the door. "Casey is someone in there with you?" her mother asked.

"No, Mom!" Casey answered, opening the door a crack. "I was just thinking of something funny."

Her mother gave her a strange look and then remembered what she'd come to say. "You have a phone call from California."

"Jo!" Casey screamed and streaked past her mom to grab the phone.

"Happy Valentine Day!" Jo shouted over the phone.

"Same to you! How are you?" Casey asked.

"I'm fine. I was sitting here thinking of those gooey, glue-covered valentines we made each other in the third grade," Jo said.

Casey chuckled as she remembered the lace doilies she had painstakingly pasted onto red construction paper. "How could I forget? What are you up to? Don't you have workout now?"

"Give me a break. It's Sunday! Even Boris rests one day a week." Jo laughed. "But I do have something to tell you."

"Well, out with it!" Casey demanded.

"Boris has been telling everyone I'm his big hopeful for the next Olympics. Can you believe that—before I've even made Elite? Boris has me doing a double with a twist off bars and it's—"

"Wow! I'm impressed!" Casey interrupted her friend. "That's fantastic!"

"I guess so. It's pretty scary, though." Jo paused. "Anyway, these news reporters from the local television station showed up at the gym to take some pictures of me."

"And now you're a star!"

"Not exactly. I fell off in the middle of my routine and smashed my chin on the mat. They even had to take me to the hospital."

"What?" Casey caught her breath. "Are you okay? Did you get hurt?"

"I'm fine now. My chin was really bruised. But it was humiliating! Krensky's big star falling flat on her face. Fortunately, Boris convinced them not to show it on TV," Jo said glumly. "I really wish I were home with you."

"Come on, Jo. Things will get better, you know that," Casey argued. "Promise me you'll keep trying your hardest."

"I will," Jo said weakly.

"Okay, now I have to tell you my news. Brett's

taking me on a picnic today!" Casey announced. She hoped that changing the subject would cheer up her friend.

"A picnic!" Jo squealed. "Where do you think you are—California?"

Casey giggled. "All I know is that it's a snow picnic."

"Are you getting serious about him?" Jo asked.

"Not really. You know I can't have a full-time boyfriend. Gymnastics has to come first." Casey sighed. "But it's hard because he's *so* cool."

"I'm glad I don't have that on my mind. Keeping up with Boris is enough. No matter what you say, I wish I was back at Flyaway. I've learned a lot here, and I know Boris is a tremendous coach, but—"

"Come on, Jo. When we're both Elites, maybe we'll get back together!" Casey told her.

"It's a deal," Jo agreed.

Casey glanced at the clock and moaned. "I've got to go. I still have to vacuum and dust before I can get ready for the picnic."

"Promise you'll write me every juicy detail?"

Giggling, Casey promised and said good-bye. After she hung up, she thought about her friend for a minute. She felt sorry for Jo, who seemed so far away and so unhappy. But nothing could cloud her enthusiasm. She was determined it would be the best Valentine's Day ever!

Two hours later, Casey and Brett climbed out of his dad's borrowed car and brushed the snow off a table in Edgeview Park along Lake Michigan.

Brett piled a heavy blanket and a picnic basket onto the table.

"What's for lunch?" Casey asked, reaching for the lid on the basket.

Quickly Brett grabbed her mittened hand. "No peeking!"

"I was just curious." Casey pretended to be offended, but she didn't pull her hand away.

"It's the usual menu for a winter picnic. Ice cream and popsicles."

Casey laughed. She wouldn't put it past him to have brought ice cream. It certainly wouldn't have needed any refrigeration, she thought as she pulled her knit scarf tighter around her neck. "What's so secretive about the lunch?"

"No secret. We just have to take a walk first." He started toward the edge of the lake, where the ice had piled up on the shore.

As Casey trudged through the snow beside him, she checked her pocket, where she'd tucked the valentine and wondered when she should give it to him. She hadn't noticed any card for her, but then, he had pockets, too.

The surface of Lake Michigan was frozen as far as Casey could see. "It would be fun to skate here," she said. She imagined herself whipping along the shore, the wind at her back giving her an extra shove.

"I don't think it's safe." He grinned down at her. "Unless you plan to jump from chunk to chunk as it cracks."

"That's me! Daredevil Benson—famous stunt skater!"

Laughing, he began to run, pulling her along.

"Hey, not so fast!" Casey protested.

"Just pretend you're skating," Brett recommended.

Casey tried to keep up as he ran. "I can't. I left my skates at home."

"You can bring them to Fletcher's Park for the skating party."

Winter Carnival! she thought. Was he finally going to ask her to go? She waited for him to go on, but he changed the subject.

"We could make a snowman," he suggested.

"No way! I can't compete with the sophomore chairman!" Casey scooped up a handful of snow and quickly formed it into a ball, which she fired at Brett, catching him on the arm.

"Not bad aim, but now it's official. You fired the first shot." He quickly packed a snowball and threw it at her as she started running.

She slid behind a big oak and stockpiled several snowballs. She peeked out from behind the tree. He was nowhere in sight.

By the time she thought to check for footprints, Brett had circled around behind her.

"Brett, no!" Casey took off, trying to reach the safety of another tree.

Brett ran after her, bombarding her with snowballs. "Bombs away!" he yelled, catching her before she could hide. One after another, he threw the snowballs, aiming at her legs and feet.

"I'll get you for this!" Casey screamed.

His last snowball sailed through the air. She ducked low, thinking it would go over her head.

As she whirled around, it caught her scarf, sending a spray of ice across her face. She gasped as the cold stung her skin.

"Oh, Casey, I'm sorry!" Brett hurried to her and began brushing off her scarf.

She tried to wipe the melting snow from her face, but her gloves were wet and caked with ice from her own snowball-making. Smiling at him, she said, "I'm okay, Brett. Really, I am."

"Here, let me." He untied her scarf and shook it. Then gently he dried her with one end. "You have very rosy cheeks," he said in a soft voice.

As Casey stood watching him, she realized they had never been so close before. She could even see the small gold streaks in his blue-gray eyes.

Brett looped her scarf back around her neck and concentrated on tying the knot carefully. When he finished, he tugged gently on both ends. But he didn't let go.

Casey thought things were moving in slow motion. She knew what was going to happen, but she didn't know if she wanted him to hurry or slow down even more.

When he looked up and their eyes met, she could feel butterflies tumble through her stomach, as though they were doing a series of back handsprings. Slowly, Brett pulled on the ends of the scarf, drawing her closer.

When his lips touched hers, Casey felt the cold disappear, replaced by a summer warmth that swirled through her. Casey reached her arms around his neck as he held her.

Brett leaned back and studied her. "Is my apology accepted?" he asked, a small smile playing at the corners of his mouth.

Casey nodded with enthusiasm. "If that was an apology, would you please throw another snowball?" She smiled at him. "Then we could start over."

"That's impossible!" Brett exclaimed.

Casey stopped smiling and turned her face away. Had she said too much? "Why is it impossible?" she asked.

"Because your mittens are dripping ice down my neck!"

Casey snatched her hands away from him. "Oh, is that right?" She flicked her icy mitten and a drop of water landed on his nose. Suddenly she shivered.

"Come on," he said, "you look frozen." Brett put his arm around her shoulders.

"I think I have snow in my boots," Casey said. Even with all her heavy clothing, the cold had begun to seep through.

He pulled her closer as they headed back to the table. "Let's dive into that picnic basket."

"I'm even hungry enough for one of those popsicles."

Brett smiled down at her. "I don't know, they might have melted." They reached the table, and Brett opened the basket. "Ta-dah!" he sang out as he produced a thermos. "Hot soup! Do you want to drink it, or soak your feet?"

"That depends. What kind is it?" Casey joked.

"Vegetable beef," he announced, and then

whipped out two coffee mugs and a couple of spoons.

Casey held the cups as he poured the steaming soup. They sat on top of the picnic table, and Brett pulled the thick blanket around them. Huddling together, they sipped their soup. After they finished, he whipped out potato chips and two tuna fish sandwiches—only slightly frozen.

Casey looked skeptically at the crispy bread. "I hope they're better than the ones at the school cafeteria."

"Trust me. I made them myself. These actually have tuna fish in them." He handed her an individual-size bag of barbecued chips. "I figured we should have something you wouldn't get at home."

Casey smiled. "Dad calls potato chips the plague."

"It must be hard living with a nutrition nut."

Casey nodded. "Make that two. Mom's just as bad."

"How does Tom manage?" Brett asked.

Giggling, Casey pulled the blanket tighter around her waist. "He sneaks food into the house." She crunched on a chip and then popped a second one in Brett's mouth.

They took turns feeding each other until the chips were gone. "This has been fun, Brett. A little crazy—but fun," Casey said.

"We'll do it again at the skating par—oops, I guess I haven't asked you yet."

Casey held her breath and made a wish. *Please*

ask me now. She stole a look at him and found him grinning at her.

"Well," he said. "Will you go?"

"Of course!" Casey squealed.

She was so excited, she felt like throwing off the blanket and doing a flip-flop. He'd finally asked her! And he'd obviously been meaning to do it all along. *Guys!* she thought. *They don't understand.* Didn't he have any idea how hard it had been for her to wait?

Brett rummaged in the picnic basket again. "To celebrate, we'll have dessert." He handed her a Snickers bar.

"Guess it can't hurt. Besides, I like them frozen." She broke off a small piece and handed it back to him.

Casey shivered and snuggled closer to him. Even knowing they were going to Winter Carnival together and sitting here next to Brett couldn't get rid of the damp cold she felt. "So, what's left in the basket? Have we finished?"

"Almost." Brett lifted the lid.

Tucked in the corner of the picnic basket, Casey could see a bundle wrapped in soft red flannel and tied with a thin white ribbon.

"I made this for you." Brett handed her the package. "I wanted to give it to you today."

Carefully, Casey unwrapped the package, and gasped. In her hands, she held his missing sculpture. A graceful gymnast doing a backbend brought the white porcelain to life. He had glazed it with a pale blue color. "Brett, this is beautiful!" she said.

Brett smiled, watching as she held it in her

hands, turning it gently to examine it from every angle. "I got the idea after you ruined *your* attempt at a gymnast," he said.

"This started out as your tire." She looked up into his smiling face. "You said it had a flat."

"I took it home to work on it."

She traced the gymnast's flowing lines. "I wish I could do things like this with clay."

"You have other things *you* do well—many things."

Casey couldn't stop looking at the gymnast, and she felt herself blushing. "Oh, Brett, thank you so much. I really love it." She sat up straighter and kissed his cheek.

She reached into her pocket and handed him his valentine. As he opened it she watched his face, trying to read his expression.

Brett didn't say anything—he just pulled her close. Hugging each other, they sat in the empty snow-covered park. Casey couldn't believe everything that had happened today: her first kiss, an invitation to Winter Carnival. . . . It wouldn't be easy fitting Brett into her schedule, but that didn't matter right now. All she wanted to do was lose herself in the magic of the afternoon.

She'd give this Valentine Day's a perfect ten.

Chapter 9

★ ★ ★ ★ ★ ★ ★ ★ ★ ★

"WELL, don't you look pleased with yourself!"

As Sarabeth bounded into the loft, Casey glanced up from her perch on the window ledge. She'd been looking down onto the gym, watching the preparation for the meet against the Aerial Gym Club. Casey could hardly believe the week had gone by so fast and that it had been six days since her picnic in the snow. With knees drawn up to her chest, she leaned back and sighed. Training hard all week had left little time just to sit and think about last Sunday's picnic with Brett.

When Casey only smiled, Sarabeth added, "If you were a cat, you'd be purring. What are you thinking about?"

"Oh, just things . . . the Elite meet." Casey didn't want to talk to Sarabeth about Brett.

"No way! No meet brings *that* kind of expression. You've been wearing that smile all week," Sarabeth pointed out.

Casey hesitated. "Maybe the meets just aren't important enough for you," she told Sarabeth.

"Oh, they're important—but they're not my whole life."

That's pretty obvious, Casey thought to herself.

"It's Brett, isn't it?" Sarabeth persisted. "How did you get him to like you so much?"

Casey swung her legs down and stood up. "I didn't do anything. And what makes you think he likes me that much?" she asked, heading for the stairs.

"I've seen the way he looks at you when you're not watching. And he *did* ask you to Winter Carnival."

Whirling around, Casey stopped. She hadn't told anyone except Monica. "How'd you know that?"

Sarabeth shrugged. "It's no secret! Everybody knows."

Sighing, Casey went downstairs with Sarabeth at her heels. She should have known Monica would spread it around school. It was hard for Monica to keep quiet when she had a juicy bit of information to share.

As they went into the gym, Sarabeth grabbed her arm. "Casey, hold up a minute. I was wondering . . . well, I need to ask you a favor." Sarabeth looked at Casey for a minute. Suddenly the smile left her face. "Never mind. This isn't a good time." And before Casey could protest, Sarabeth had gone into the locker room.

Now, what was that all about? Casey wondered. Shrugging, she went to find Monica.

* * *

Casey felt her stomach fall as she watched Sarabeth go through her bars routine. She'd seen more concentration in a beginning gymnast! Sarabeth was going through her moves too fast, as if she didn't care whether her team won the meet or not.

When Sarabeth dismounted, Casey stormed off to the last rotation. She was mad, and she didn't care who knew it. She threw her duffel bag under her chair. How could Sarabeth put the team in jeopardy yet again? And why did Chip continue to have Sarabeth go last on bars?

Casey already knew the answer. He was betting Sarabeth would come through with one of her extraordinary performances. Casey sighed. She didn't understand her teammate at all. How could she be so brilliant one time and so mediocre the next?

Monica nudged Casey. "Take it easy! Don't let her get to you. You don't want to blow your own floor ex."

"I know," Casey said, "but she makes me so mad! It's not fair to the team. She knew these Aerial girls were tough."

While Casey tried to calm down, she concentrated on watching Tracy, Shannon, and Holly's floor routines. She'd worry about Sarabeth later. But she wasn't going to sit back and ignore it any longer. After the meet, she'd talk to Monica. Something had to be done.

Somehow, she got through her own routine, but Casey knew it hadn't been her best. She slumped into her chair, and gave a thumbs-up to Monica, who stood in her beginning pose at the edge of the mat.

Monica's floor exercise was dazzling. Chip had choreographed the routine to take advantage of her gracefulness. She floated through split leaps that seemed to defy gravity, and her last tumbling run with its double full twist showed that she had the strength and power she needed to be a good gymnast.

When the team scores were announced, it was another close one, but this time the Flyaways hadn't been able to pull it out. Even Casey's high-scoring layout on the beam hadn't been enough to ensure the win.

Her first place individual ribbon for beam and second place All-Around didn't make Casey feel any better. The team was more important—and now all their hopes for an undefeated season were gone.

In the locker room, Casey sat down next to Monica. "What are we going to do?" she said.

"With our illustrious teammate, you mean?" Monica looked around the room. "Where is she now?"

"I don't know, but I think we should talk to her," Casey said.

Monica nodded. "It might help. Maybe we can catch her at school on Monday or here, before practice."

"She'd never arrive early. She can hardly make it on time."

"Okay, you're right," Monica agreed. "We'll keep our eyes open, and the first time we see her alone, we'll pounce."

Smiling at Monica, Casey began to get her things

out of her locker. "It may not do any good—but we *have* to try."

Monica swung her team bag over her shoulder. "My mom and dad are taking me to lunch. Want to come along?" she asked.

"No, thanks. I don't feel like doing anything right now. I don't know why this bothers me so much, but it does."

"I'll call you later," Monica promised. "You were great today anyway!"

"Thanks," Casey said, trying to smile. "So were you."

Monday, at school, Casey spotted Sarabeth in the cafeteria at lunchtime. Sarabeth waved and then sat down to eat with a group of cheerleaders. Determined to set up a time she and Monica could talk to Sarabeth, Casey started toward the table.

A few feet away, she stopped. The girls seemed excited about something, and Sarabeth was in the midst of it all. Shrugging, Casey decided to wait. She'd catch her later at the gym.

But Sarabeth didn't show up for workout that day.

The next day, Casey tried to find out what had happened, but Sarabeth managed to avoid both her and Monica all day.

But it didn't take long for them to figure out what she was up to when an announcement came over the loudspeaker just before they left for the gym: "Congratulations to our cheerleaders! Fair-field's pep squad took first place in a citywide competition in Kennilworth yesterday. We're very proud of them!"

"So that's it!" Casey said aloud. Sarabeth had cut workout to go to a cheerleading competition. She could hardly believe it.

Casey remembered the time she'd skipped practice to go to the football game with Brett. But that had been after an argument with her father, when he coached her at the high school. Because of a misunderstanding, she thought he had kicked her off the team.

"What's wrong?" Monica asked as they headed out the front door of the school.

"I just found out why Sarabeth skipped practice. She went to that cheering thing in Kennilworth," Casey told her friend.

Monica whistled. "So that's why she's been avoiding us all day!"

"She really has a lot of nerve," Casey said.

"She has more nerve than a sky diver," Monica agreed.

"Don't tell *her* that," Casey muttered. "She'll take up that hobby, too. Monica, we have to talk to her! The team is at stake. We won't win the Zone Championship unless she's performing her best. And what if Chip kicks her off the team?"

"I know," Monica said. "Let's catch her after practice. She won't dare skip two days in a row."

"Okay," Casey agreed.

Casey sat in the back of the locker room, waiting for Monica to come in with Sarabeth. Now that it was actually time for their big talk, Casey was be-

ginning to chicken out. It probably wouldn't do any
good, and Sarabeth might compete even worse,
just to get back at them.

Casey sighed. Sarabeth could have been a good
friend. She was a lot of fun, and she'd arrived at a
time when both she and Monica were feeling a
void because Jo was gone.

The door to the gym opened, and Casey heard
Monica's voice. "Casey should be back here."

"What's the big deal? Why's everything so secretive?" Sarabeth asked as the two girls came around
the corner. "Will somebody please tell me what's
going on?" She sounded angry.

"We want to talk to you about the team," Casey
said.

Cocking her head, Sarabeth studied Casey. Then
she sat down next to her. "Okay, what do you want
to know?"

"Well . . . we've been watching you at workout
and the meets, and we don't think you really care
about the team, whether we win or lose."

Sarabeth's eyes narrowed. "What makes you the
expert on how much I care about something?"

Casey looked to Monica for help. Monica cleared
her throat. "What Casey means is, well, we don't
think you really want to be here at Flyaway."

"You even cut workout to go to that cheerleading competition to watch your friends," Casey
added.

Sarabeth glared at Casey. "How'd you know
that?"

Monica shook her head. "We just figured it out
after we heard the announcement about it. Every-

body knows you weren't home sick, and we saw
you at school, hanging out with the cheerleaders."

"Well, you're right!" Sarabeth jumped to her feet.
"I hate the Flyaway Gym Club! I hate gymnastics!
I hate you!" She stopped shouting and sat down on
the bench. "No, I don't hate you . . . just the gymnastics." She closed her eyes and let out a long
sigh.

Exchanging glances with Monica, Casey felt frus-
trated. What had they gotten into? She reached out
to touch Sarabeth, but she jerked her arm away.
"Sarabeth, what's wrong? Why are you at the gym
if you hate it?" Casey asked quietly.

Sarabeth opened her eyes and sat up straighter.
"Ask my parents. *They're* the ones who should be
here."

"What do your parents have to do with you being on the team?" Monica asked.

"They're the ones that insist I do gymnastics. I'm
supposed to develop discipline. They think it'll keep
me busy . . . and away from boys and any kind of
social life." Sarabeth wrinkled up her nose. "They
figure that if I'm so involved with gymnastics, I
won't have time for anything else. And they're
right!"

"But you're such a good gymnast—when you
want to be," Casey said.

"That's the trouble! I thought if I screwed up half
the time, Chip would kick me off the team." She
looked down at the floor. "But he's been so nice.
He's given me dozens of chances." She sighed, then
continued, "It's different with you guys. You have

dreams to go to the top in gymnastics. I don't. All I ever wanted to do was be a cheerleader!"

"A cheerleader!" Monica and Casey said in unison.

"Couldn't you just tell your folks you'd rather do that?" Casey asked.

Sarabeth laughed. "I did. My dad acted like I'd hit him in the stomach. No daughter of his was going to be an airhead cheerleader!"

Casey couldn't imagine her parents making her do something she didn't care about. She wondered what her dad would have done if she'd really quit the gymnastics team at Fairfield. Her older sister, Barbara, hadn't ever been a gymnast, and that was okay with him.

Casey could imagine what a terrible strain it would be to pretend to like something, all for your parents' benefit. "I understand your problem," she told Sarabeth. "And I can sympathize with you. But *please* don't ruin our team's chances. It's not fair to the rest of us."

"I guess I have only been thinking of myself," Sarabeth admitted.

Monica nodded her head. "You sure have. But you can starting thinking of the team—right now."

"At least give us until after the Zone Championship," Casey pleaded. "Then maybe we can think of some way to help you convince your parents to let you be a cheerleader."

Sarabeth agreed to work hard until after the Class I season ended. When they left the gym, Casey felt a lot better. She was glad that they had finally spoken up and shared their concern. Maybe it wouldn't solve anything, but at least they would still have a chance to win the Zone meet.

Chapter 10

★★★★★★★★★★

CASEY could not sit still. It had been a good workout, and now, as Chip talked about plans for the Elite Championships, she was getting more and more excited. She'd been counting forever; first the years till she could go, then the weeks, and finally, it was down to days.

Now, he was actually talking about their travel plans. And she was going to get her chance to prove she could do it—to make Elite status and look forward to being selected for one of the national teams.

"First, we need to get through the Class I season. The Zone meet is a big one for all of us." He looked at each girl, his eyes settling on Sarabeth, who was busy studying her fingernails.

Chip shook his head and continued. "I want you to know what's going to happen at the Elite meet. We'll fly to Oakland on Monday. That'll give us two days to work out on their equipment and get the feel of a new place—plus catch up on any jet lag."

"Can those of us not in it come to watch?" Shannon asked.

"If any of the team wants to go with us, we'd like to have you—as long as you can afford the plane fare. Several of you will be there in the next couple of years, and it will give you a chance to check it out."

Casey looked at her teammates, most of whom were as excited as if they were competing, too. She hoped they would all come along to cheer on her and Monica.

Casey looked for her best friend, but Monica wasn't sitting with the team. She'd been right there a minute ago. Casey hoped nothing was wrong.

"We'll stay in the hotel and then return to Chicago in the morning, after the Saturday-night finals." Chip paused. "So there you have it! Check with your parents to see if you can swing it, and join us if you can."

A whole week, Casey thought. A whole week away from school—and Brett. She wished he could see her in the biggest event of her life. Her parents would fly to Oakland in time for the optionals, which was great—but she still wanted Brett to be there.

When Chip dismissed them, the rest of the team sat on the mats discussing the meet, but Casey hurried into the locker room to see if Monica was all right. As she left the group, she heard Chip ask Sarabeth to come to his office. Casey knew Chip would make her pay for cutting workout.

Casey found her friend standing at her locker, already dressed. Monica turned away, but not before Casey saw her red eyes.

"Monica!" she cried. "What's wrong? You've been crying!"

"No, I haven't." Monica wiped a tear away as she turned back to Casey.

Confused, Casey asked, "Did you get hurt during practice? I didn't see you fall."

Shaking her head, Monica looked at the floor. "No, I'm fine."

"But you missed all the details about the Elite meet," Casey said. "We get a whole day and a half in Oakland to warm up before it starts."

"I'm not going to the meet," Monica announced.

"What?" Casey shrieked. "But we've planned for so long—you can't give up now!"

Tears ran down Monica's face. "It wasn't my decision—it was Chip's. He doesn't want me to compete this year."

"But why?"

Monica gulped. "He said if I didn't do well this year, the judges would remember, and it would be harder the next time." She threw herself into Casey's outstretched arms. "Casey, I . . . I can't stand it! We've always counted . . . on going together," Monica gasped out between sobs.

"I can't believe this is happening!" Standing there, hugging her best friend, Casey didn't know what else to say. She knew Chip had to have given this a lot of thought and that he was probably right, but still, his decision was devastating.

"You and Jo will have to go on without me," Monica choked out.

Jo would also be competing in the meet at the Oakland Auditorium. They had planned to get together and celebrate afterward. "Monica, you have to come!" Casey urged her. "Chip wants the whole team to come and watch if they can afford it."

"He—he already told me he wants me to go. But I don't know if I can stand to sit there and watch you compete and me not. . . ." Monica broke into sobs again.

Casey guided Monica onto one of the benches and sat down beside her. She put her arm around Monica's shoulders and squeezed tightly. For years, they had dreamed about going to the Elite meet. It had never occurred to Casey that they might not all make it. She shuddered, trying to imagine how she would feel if she were the one being left behind. It didn't seem fair, with the Olympics just over two years away.

"Casey! Wait up!"

Turning around, Casey saw Sarabeth running down the hall after her. It was Wednesday morning, and Casey had just left her algebra class. After Chip had asked to talk to Sarabeth the day before, Casey had been dying of curiosity.

"Hi, Sarabeth!" Casey said as her teammate caught up to her. "You look pretty happy. What's up?"

Sarabeth took a quick breath. "It happened! Chip finally kicked me off the team!"

Casey's eyes widened. "Just like that?"

"Well, we talked about it." Sarabeth grinned. "We decided it was—what did he say?—mutually acceptable."

"And I don't need to ask if you're psyched about it."

"Oh, Casey, I'm so glad I don't have to spend every afternoon at the gym."

Casey could hardly believe that she was really off the team. "Won't you miss it at all?" she asked.

For a second, Sarabeth paused. "I think I will miss it some." Then her face brightened again. "But not the grind. I'll be able to go to parties and date boys and all those other fun things. That'll make up for it!"

"What about your parents?"

"We had a pretty big fight." Sarabeth made a face. "Chip called them and told them I wasn't doing well at Flyaway, that it wasn't the right place for me. My dad almost launched himself into orbit."

"You didn't get grounded for life or anything?"

Sarabeth laughed. "No, fortunately they don't believe in capital punishment. But they're already looking for *another* activity for me."

"*They're* looking for you?" Casey shook her head.

"Yeah, but this time I'm going to put up a fight. It's about time we talked about it," Sarabeth said.

Suddenly Casey had a feeling she would miss Sarabeth. The team would be better off without her because she was so inconsistent, but she was fun, if a little crazy at times. Casey smiled. "It'll seem strange not having you there—you know, coming in late. . . ." she teased.

"Thanks, Casey. I'll miss you guys, too. But we'll see each other in art class."

"Yeah, the two square pegs lost in a class of talent. Maybe we can share some bad jokes," Casey suggested.

"I don't suppose you'd like to share Brett?"

Casey started to protest, but a fiery glance at Sarabeth produced a peal of laughter, and Casey knew she was only kidding.

Laughing, Casey started toward the student store, where she was meeting Brett. As she turned down the corridor, she saw him leaning against the wall waiting for her.

Now she and Brett walked to several classes together. The rest of the time, she had to settle for phone calls after workout, and art class, to talk to him.

Brett had wanted to start eating lunch with Casey, but she couldn't do that to Monica. They had always shared lunch together. Casey didn't want to give up that special time.

"Hi, Michelangelo!"

Casey shifted her books and smiled at Brett. "You're the Michelangelo now. How's the snow sculpture?"

"All set. We just need lots of new snow."

"We could do an Indian rain dance."

"Rain!" He threw up his hands. "That would ruin the whole thing!"

Casey laughed. "Well, a snow dance, then."

Brett looked smug. "We've already planned to do that. Pretty powerful chief coming to conduct the ceremony." He folded his arms across his chest, Indian style. "It's going to snow on the sophomore section of the school yard only."

Casey nodded. "I should have known."

"After the judging, we'll go to the ice skating

party. I talked to Derek, and it's all set. We'll go with them," Brett said.

"I hope we can make it there before they announce the winners. Chip won't let me out early so close to the Elite meet."

"Not to worry! Derek will pick you up at the gym right at eight," Brett told her. "Just make sure you take all your stuff to workout."

"I'm really looking forward to the skating party. I can't believe so much is happening. First, the Zone meet and then the carnival and then the Elite Championships. I'm so excited, I can't stand it!" Casey exclaimed.

Brett laughed as he left her at history class, and headed for the room next door.

That afternoon, Casey worked with Holly on her vault, helping to perfect her run and takeoff from the springboard. Casey's own vaults had gone well, and she could feel her confidence building. With the Zone Championship coming up that weekend, she was getting anxious.

To be winners, they'd have to defeat the Aerial Gym Club. She hoped they'd be ready.

She moved over to the balance beam to finish her workout. Before starting, she sat down on the mat and watched Monica. "It's looking good," she said as Monica finished her dismount.

Monica shook her head. "It's coming, but the mount is still wobbly. I must have done it twenty times today."

Casey was worried about her friend; Monica had been so depressed over Chip's decision to make her wait a year to try for Elite. But right then, Casey had to concentrate on getting herself ready for the Zone competition.

"I'll be glad to go home. I'm starving!" Casey said, rubbing her stomach.

"So, what's new? My stomach always growls through my last rotation." Monica grimaced.

Laughing, Casey went to the low beam and ran through the layout several times. Then she lined up the springboard for her mount. She completed the routine two more times and saw Chip nod his approval.

She looked at the clock. Seven-fifteen. She wondered what her mom had made for dinner. She hoped it would be good, but she could eat anything right then. In answer, a gurgle rumbled from her stomach. She and Shannon, who was spotting her, giggled, and Casey went back to the end of the beam to start again.

Completing a high leap and a turn, she set up for her back handspring. Out of the corner of her eye, she saw Monica talking to Chip. *Concentrate!* she told herself. She threw herself backward into the flip and pushed off, stretching her body into the layout position.

When she landed, her foot came down a little off to the right. She wobbled and tried to bend forward at the waist to catch her balance, but it was no use. She fell off backwards, hitting her head on the base of the beam. The room wavered, then went black, as if the lights had been shut off.

The last thing Casey remembered was Monica's horrified face.

Chapter 11

* * * * * * * * * *

CASEY opened her eyes. From her position under the beam, she saw a sea of faces peering down at her. Quickly, she closed her eyes again, as things began to spin around her.

"Casey! Casey! Can you hear me?" Chip called.

Casey looked again, and this time he came into focus. She rubbed her head. "What happened?"

"Thank God you're okay." He let out a long breath.

As Casey struggled to get up, a pain shot through her head and she lay down again. "My head is exploding."

"Don't try to get up yet." Chip tenderly checked her over for breaks. "Can you move everything?"

Still lying flat, she rotated her ankles and bent her knees. "I think I'm okay."

Shannon knelt beside her. "Oh, Casey, I was so scared. I thought you were dead."

Casey tried to smile, but even that hurt her head.

She reached for Shannon's hand. "Good thing I'm not. We still have that Zone meet."

Casey's comment broke the tension, and everyone started to laugh. Soon they were all sharing their views of the accident. Chip excused the team early and carefully helped Casey to her feet. When Monica and Shannon didn't move, he asked, "Aren't you part of the team I just dismissed?"

"I can't *leave* her!" Monica cried.

Chip laughed. "All right. I'll run you both home on the way to the emergency room. Get on her other side and help me. We'll take her to my van."

"What can I do?" Shannon danced around, anxious to help.

"Aspirin," Casey demanded, "lots of them."

"Not till we see the doctor," Chip said. "Monica, get your stuff—Casey's, too—and meet us in the parking lot."

They stretched Casey out in the back of the van. Monica wanted to hold her head, but Casey thought it would feel better lying flat. Turning and twisting in the front seat, both of her teammates tried to look back at her and talk. Finally Chip dropped them off. "Those two are a couple of jumping beans," he said.

"They're just worried about me," Casey said from the back.

"You gave us all a scare."

"Me, too!"

Chip drove to the hospital, and after he signed her in, he called Casey's parents. Fifteen minutes later, the Bensons walked into the emergency room. Chip explained to her parents what had happened, and Casey's mom stayed with her while the doctor checked out her injury.

Once the doctor had left, Chip came in and sat down on the edge of the bed. "How are you feeling?" he asked.

"Not so good." Casey tried to smile. "But the doctor thinks I'll be fine after a good night's sleep."

"Casey . . . I have to tell you this." He looked at her and shook his head. "We're taking the layout out of your routine for Zone."

"Oh, no." Casey tried to protest further, but her head hurt too much to think.

"I won't take a chance on your getting hurt again. We need you for Zone, and now we just want to concentrate on getting you healthy enough to compete." He patted her shoulder. "I know you're disappointed, but we'll go back to the layout for the Elite meet, I promise."

Casey nodded and closed her eyes. She knew she'd be disappointed in the morning, but that night she just wanted to sleep.

On the Saturday morning of the Zone Championship, the locker room at Willowbrook was surprisingly quiet, even with nine teams dressing. Everyone seemed to be speaking in whispers. The tension was high.

As they went into the gym, Casey looked around the large building with the skylight built into the ceiling. Portable bleachers had been assembled along one side of the gym, and a second-story viewing area held several rows of chairs. Only a few spectators had arrived to watch the warmups, but Casey knew the stands would fill up soon. This was an important meet, and it would draw lots of parents and friends.

A gold balloon bobbed near the ceiling. Casey's eyes followed the long string down to the balloon's owner. "Brett!" she burst out, surprised to see him. She hadn't asked him to come, because she thought he'd be working.

As much as she wanted to talk to him, she had to be satisfied knowing he was there. Chip didn't let any of his team mingle with the crowd—not even with parents—before a meet. But when Brett saw Casey staring at him, he flashed a victory sign.

Checking to see that Chip wasn't looking, she waved back.

"Brett's in the bleachers." Casey smiled as she nodded toward where he sat.

"I wish Derek could have come. He wanted to, but he had to work."

"Brett usually works on Saturdays, too," Casey said. The idea that he'd taken time off to watch her pleased Casey, but she was determined not to show off for them the way Sarabeth had when guys had come to the meets.

Monica sat down next to Casey. "The Aerial Gym Club girls are telling everyone they're going to beat us today," she whispered.

"Then they'll be disappointed," Casey said. "I just know we're going to win." Casey had completely recovered from her accident. She'd had a headache the next day, but that was it. She was glad—she wouldn't have missed this for the world.

The meet proceeded at a rapid pace through the

first three rotations. Both the Flyaway and Aerial gymnasts were competing well and out in front of the other teams, but the Aerial Gym Club girls had edged ahead in points. The Flyaways were a close second.

Casey began to worry. Her team still had the beam as their last event, and the Aerials had only to score reasonably well on their vaults. Beam was a bad event to have last, because the other events were distracting—especially the music from the floor exercise. Casey wasn't sure they could pull it off. When Holly fell off the beam, their chances of winning dropped even further.

Next to Casey, Monica turned in her chair to watch the vault. She winced every time an Aerial girl completed a good one. "If only you still had your layout—then we might have a chance," she said softly.

"I still have it. I've been sneaking in a little practice whenever Chip wasn't there," she murmured to Monica.

She looked at her rotation. There were still three more gymnasts from her team who had to perform before she did. Monica would perform right before her and would probably score well. If Casey included her layout, the judges would have to score it better—if she landed it.

Casey got up and went over to where Chip stood, closer to the beam. "Coach," she began. "With the scores escalating, Monica's got a chance to score pretty well. If I put my layout combination back in, I'd get a great score."

"No way! You haven't been practicing! It's too dangerous," Chip argued.

"But Chip, I *have* been doing it," Casey protested.

Chip stared at her a minute, but she could see he was thinking about it. Finally he asked, "Have you done it since the accident?"

Casey felt her face turn red. She smiled sheepishly and nodded. "I didn't want to lose it. I have to have it ready for the Elite meet."

"No, it's too iffy." He shook his head and threw up his hands. "Don't argue. Just do a good job on your regular routine."

Casey went back and sat down next to Monica. "He said no."

Monica gave her a hug. "We just might make it anyway."

Casey nodded. "Listen, I need a good score from you, okay?"

Monica grinned. "I'll do my best!"

"Go for it!" Casey said as Monica got up to get ready for her turn.

The other events finished, and the gymnasts gathered on the mats to watch the last two girls on beam. A hush fell over the gym as Monica mounted the beam. She did a fantastic routine, and the judges gave it an 8.5, the best score of the afternoon.

The score between the two teams narrowed. *Win or lose, it's all on my shoulders*, Casey thought. She knew if she added the layout combination and made it, they would win.

As she started toward the beam, Chip called to her. "Casey!"

Casey looked over her shoulder at her coach.

"Do it!"

Casey felt a rush of relief. She signaled for quiet, and the room fell silent. She was glad for all her experience in past competitions. She visualized her whole routine in her mind, then saluting the judge, she punched the springboard and sprang onto the beam.

She sailed through the beginning with ease. As she neared the layout combination, she concentrated even harder. *Stay on and keep centered,* she told herself. *Don't let them down now.* When she threw herself into the back handspring, she reached her hands for the beam, immediately launching into her layout, her body arched above the narrow wooden strip. She landed solidly with only a tiny wobble. The crowd gasped and burst into applause. But that didn't bother Casey now. She was on a roll, and all she had was her pirouette turn and the setup for her dismount. She landed her double twist, and the crowd went wild. She had done it!

Casey saluted the judge again. If she could come through now, so soon after her injury, she could do it again in the Elite Championships meet. She waved at the crowd and sent a special smile to Brett.

Monica and the rest of her team quickly surrounded her. "I knew you could do it! I just knew it!" Monica said, giving her a big hug.

Shannon hugged her, too. "I think I held my breath during your whole routine," she said.

Behind the team, Casey saw Chip grinning at her. She untangled herself from her friends and went over to where he waited. Unexpectedly, he scooped Casey up and spun her around. "You did it! Thank goodness I decided to let you try it." He let her down gently. "Still sorry you aren't off competing in California?"

"No way! I'm here to stay! And thanks, Chip. It was my best ever."

"I think you pushed us into the win. You really were the star," Chip told her, smiling. To Casey, those words were magic.

When the scores were tallied, the Flyaway Gym Club had won the meet by three-tenths of a point. To whistles and cheers, the whole team crowded onto the six blocks to receive their ribbons and the trophy for the club.

After the awards were given, parents and friends drifted down from the bleachers to offer the team their congratulations.

Casey looked around for Brett and spotted him sitting at the top of the bleachers, still watching her.

Grinning, she bounded up the stairs. Brett stood up and took her hand, tying the balloon around her wrist as he'd done after each meet he'd seen. Then he put his arm around her shoulders. "You were great!"

Casey lifted her arm into the air. "I feel like I could float away. Thanks for being here!" She gave him a quick hug. "But aren't you supposed to be working?"

"I switched with the night shift so I could come. Unfortunately, that means I can't catch a movie with you tonight." He gave an exaggerated sigh. "Hippo's Burgers keep calling. But at least I have all of next weekend off for Winter Carnival."

Casey shivered in anticipation.

After Brett left, Casey changed, and the team rode back to the Flyaway Gym Club in Chip's van. Casey wondered how Chip ever drove with all the noise from five enthusiastic girls, excited over winning the Zone Championship. She was sure he couldn't hear himself think.

"I'll treat you all to pizza!" Chip shouted over the noisy voices.

"Great!" They all yelled back.

"You're fantastic, Chip!" Shannon said.

"No, you're the ones who were fantastic." Chip got off the expressway at the Fairfield exit. "We'll make a quick stop at the club so you can get your gear."

Casey thought the gym looked lonely as they walked into the empty club. With classes for young gymnasts over for the day, it was strangely quiet. A colorful banner, with the sloppy handwritten message "Good Luck Class I's" hung crookedly on one wall. It all looked sad to Casey, somehow.

Suddenly she thought of Jo and wondered how she'd done in her Zone meet out in California. Boris's gym had competed a week ago, but so far,

Casey and Monica hadn't heard any results from their friend.

Chip came up behind Casey. "What happened to your smile?" he asked.

"Hi. I was just thinking about Jo."

"Why don't we call and give her the news?" Chip suggested. He punched Casey's arm lightly.

"Oh, Chip, could we?"

"Go get the rest of the team while I look up the number." He headed for his office.

Casey called the team, and they crowded around Chip while he dialed Jo's number.

"Hello, Jo? This is Chip, here at Flyaway. . . . It's good to hear you, too. Say, I've got an office full of screaming women waiting to talk to you."

As Chip handed the phone to Monica, Casey stepped back to let the others go first. She listened to Monica tell her about her role in the win. Bits of conversation were shouted into the receiver by the other girls. Finally, it was Casey's turn.

"Jo! We did it!" she shouted.

"Casey, I'm so proud of you. I wish I could have been there to compete along with you guys," Jo said.

"Don't get all gushy on me. Tell me how you did!" Casey urged.

"Krensky's won, too."

"You must have won bars, then, with that super dismount. With that amount of difficulty, you must have blown them away!"

For a few seconds Jo was silent, then she gave a nervous laugh. "I did great on bars, but—"

"What's wrong?"

Jo gave a loud sigh. "Well, now that I've gotten back to doing the dismount, Boris is pushing me to add more to it."

"Jo, you can do it! Just think how good you'll be at the Elite meet. You're going to wipe me off the floor," Casey predicted.

"I doubt it! I still wish I was back with you guys." Jo paused.

"We miss you, Jo, a lot." Casey looked up to see Chip pointing to his watch. "Gotta go. Chip's going to make me work off this call in sit-ups."

Casey hung up and tried to shake off the uneasy feeling she had about Jo. Ever since her friend had left for California, she had seemed incredibly unhappy. Maybe if they'd been out there together, things would have been different. Casey would have been able to help her though the rough times.

The more she thought about it, the happier she was to be at home, working with Chip, training for the Elite Trials. Especially now that they were Zone champs!

Chapter 12

"WOULD you two settle down!" Chip yelled across the gym at Casey and Monica, who were working together on the balance beam.

Casey sighed. How could she concentrate, when that night was the skating party, and Derek would be there in an hour to pick them up to head for the park? She tingled with excitement. Sometime during the evening, they'd find out if Brett had won the snow sculpture contest. "This has been the longest workout of my life," she said to Monica, who stood on the beam.

Monica shook her head. "I must have looked at the clock a hundred times."

"I can't wait to know who won the contest."

Monica grinned. "Do I detect you're not a hundred percent with the freshman class?"

"Well . . ."

"I can't believe it—a traitor." Monica hopped off the beam to give Casey a turn.

"Girls!" Chip shouted. "What are we holding over there—a mouth marathon?"

Waving at Chip, Casey said, "Guess we better get back to work." She climbed onto the beam and began to run through the easier elements in her routine.

Shannon walked over. "Chip sent me to work beam with you, Monica. He wants to see you, Casey."

"Uh-oh." Casey rolled her eyes. "It's lecture time!"

Monica tried to imitate Chip. "You're not applying yourself, Casey, and there's an awfully big meet coming up."

As she left, Casey made a face at her friend. "The trouble is—he's right. I'll have to double up from here on in."

Chip motioned Casey to the front of his office. "Hi there," he said. "Look, have you decided you're not going to the Elite meet?"

"I'm sorry, Chip—I'm trying. I guess I shouldn't be going to Winter Carnival, but it's the biggest thing all winter at school and—"

Chip interrupted her. "You're going to have to work late every night for the next two weeks. You know that, don't you?"

Casey could see that his stern look was softening. "Yes. I promise I'll concentrate more after tonight."

"Since both of you seem to be wasting your time here tonight, why don't you take off now?" Chip suggested. "And have a good time."

"Oh, Chip, thank you!" Casey gave him a hug.

"You'll pay for it, though. I'm going to work your tail off next week," he threatened.

Casey nodded. "Fair enough."

"I should have let you go even earlier, but there's a special reason why I didn't," Chip said, his eyes now sparkling with excitement instead of anger.

"What is it?"

He glanced at the clock. "You'll see in a few minutes."

Curious, Casey went back to the beam and tried to concentrate on her routine. It was no use. She just couldn't settle down.

Then she heard a commotion. At the gym door, Chip and Shannon and Tracy were talking at the top of their lungs. Finishing her dismount, Casey wondered what it was all about. As she headed for the others, she stopped, then began to run.

Jo was standing in the doorway!

"Jo!" Casey screamed, grabbing her friend into a hug. "I can't believe it's you! And with a suntan— in the wintertime!"

Jo grinned. "I got to the beach once or twice."

"When did you get here?" Monica shouted as she raced up from behind. While she hugged Jo, the rest of the team crowded around, everybody talking at once.

Jo beamed as she hugged her friends. "I came right from the airport. I couldn't wait to see you!"

Finally, Casey untangled herself from the group. "Jo, what are you *doing* here?" she asked.

"I'm home," Jo said.

"You're what? You mean you left Krensky's?"

"But you were a star there!" Monica protested.

Jo sighed. "Look, you guys, I needed to come back here. I just couldn't stand the stress of living out there. Maybe I won't make it, but I had to come home."

Casey caught Chip's eye, and she grabbed Jo's arm. "You can make it from the Flyaway. It's all in your mind." Over Jo's head, she saw Chip's grin, and he nodded. Turning back to Jo, she said, "We'll make it together."

"Thanks, Casey." Jo whirled around to include the rest of the team. "I can't wait to work out with all of you again. Hey, Casey, can you and Monica spend the night at my house? It'll be just like old times."

Drawing a quick breath, Casey exchanged a pained look with Monica. Jo had surprised them with her return, and now they wouldn't be able to share her first night home. Derek would be picking them up in a few minutes.

"What's wrong?" Jo asked. "You two look like you've seen a ghost."

Monica signaled for Casey to explain. With a lump in her throat, Casey tried to find a way to tell Jo that they had plans for the whole weekend. "Tonight is the beginning of Winter Carnival, and we're going to the skating party."

"Great! I hope I can find my skates!"

Casey and Monica exchanged looks. Of course, Jo would assume they'd all go together. They'd been a threesome for as long as she could remember.

"Jo . . . we can't go with you. We both have dates!" Monica blurted.

"Oh!" Jo's eyes widened as a hurt look spread

across her face. "That's okay. We have the rest of the weekend to catch up." She tried to smile, but it came out forced.

Casey didn't have the heart to tell Jo that they'd be going to the basketball game the next night.

Chip clapped his hands for attention. "Jo will show us everything she's learned tomorrow." he looked at his returning gymnast. "You'll be here for workout in the morning, won't you?"

"I wouldn't miss it!" The smile came back to Jo's face. "It's going to be so good to be part of this team again."

Casey flashed Chip a thank-you smile for helping her out of a sticky situation and put her arm around her friend. "Jo, I missed you so much. And we're dying to hear all about California."

"Let's have lunch after workout tomorrow," Monica said from her other side.

"Pizza!" Tracy shouted.

"Sandwiches at the Natural Earth," Chip corrected.

Hugging Jo, Casey whispered, "I'm sorry Winter Carnival had to spoil your homecoming."

"It's okay," Jo replied. "We have lots of time."

Casey just wished that she could do something to ease Jo's disappointment. The next day, they'd have to make it up to her.

As they pulled into the parking lot at Fletcher's Park, Casey saw Brett leaning against a tree, with his skates thrown over his shoulder. When he saw the car, he hurried over and took Casey's skates for her.

"I thought you'd never get here," he said as he linked his arm through hers.

"Have they started? Do you know anything about the snow sculptures?" Casey asked.

Brett grinned. "You're awfully anxious to know if the freshmen beat me."

"Brett! You know that isn't true!"

Reaching the skating pond, Casey saw dozens of kids from Fairfield speeding across the ice. Just beyond, more students sat on logs around a huge bonfire that sent flames and sparks into the air. The senior class had set up large pots of hot chocolate and platters of cookies near the fire.

Brett and Casey sat down on a bench along the edge of the pond and laced up their skates. Brett tied Casey's extra tight, and they started out to skate together.

It was Casey's first time skating this winter, and as she moved across the ice, her ankles felt wobbly. "Why does everyone think the balance beam is hard? It's a whole lot easier than standing up on ice," she said.

Brett took her arm to steady her. "It takes a few turns around to get going."

Brett was right, and soon Casey was keeping up with everyone else. But when she joined a crack-the-whip line, Brett had to grab her so she wouldn't fly into the fence. "Maybe you're not ready for this yet," he said as he led her to the fire to warm up. "I'll get us some hot chocolate."

Casey found a seat on a big log near the fire. As she made herself comfortable, Sarabeth came over to join her. "Hi, Casey. I wanted to wish you luck."

"Hi, Sarabeth! We've missed you at the gym. What are you doing with all your time these days?"

Sarabeth shifted a package that was tucked under her arm. "Just kicking back—hanging out with some kids."

Casey gave an exaggerated sigh. "That sounds good about now."

"I bet you don't even *know* the word *relax* these days."

"Oh, how right you are! I've been at the gym six hours every day, but"— Casey dug a hole in the hard ground with her skate blade—"we leave in nine days."

Sarabeth held out the package. "I brought you these. Maybe they'll bring you luck."

Curious, Casey quickly undid the brown-paper wrapping. She gasped. Inside were two of Sarabeth's specially dyed leotards. She rubbed her fingers across the soft pastel colors. "Are you sure you want to give these to me?"

"Yeah. I won't be needing them anymore. But you don't *have* to take them to the meet."

"Oh, but I will. I'll wear them during optionals." Casey hoped that by wearing them, she could also take on a little of Sarabeth's explosive power on the vault.

Sarabeth jumped to her feet. "I gotta go. I hope you wow 'em, Casey." She paused. "I really want you to make it."

"I'm going to try. See you when I get back. And don't bother to look after Brett while I'm gone," she said, giving her friend a playful poke.

Brett returned with two steaming cups of hot

chocolate piled high with miniature marshmallows. As he sat down, the senior class president went to the loudspeaker. "Everybody! Listen up! We're going to announce the winners of the snow sculpture now."

"Sarabeth just left," Casey said as the crowd began to gather around them. "She brought me a good luck package—two of the leotards her mom made."

"That Sarabeth. She's unbelievable!"

Casey didn't answer. She stared at the flames that gave a soft glow to the snowy scene. Why did she keep wondering how Brett felt about Sarabeth? She didn't think he really liked the other girl, but she still had occasional doubts.

Brett leaned closer so that he could see her face. "What's wrong, Casey?"

Casey busied herself picking snow off her mittens. Taking a deep breath, she said, "I thought you might like her."

"Sarabeth? You've got to be kidding!" Brett reached for her hand. "What ever made you think that?"

Looking into Brett's eyes, Casey pushed all her doubts away. "I guess it was dumb," she said with a sigh of relief.

"I'm flattered that you were jealous," he said, grinning at her.

The senior president started announcing the awards, and the freshmen won last place. The ninth graders cheered anyway, and Casey joined in while Brett shook his head and gave her an amused smile. "See what happens when you don't have time to be part of the committee?" he said.

"But then, *you* would have lost," she countered.

After the juniors claimed third place, the senior president paused to tease the crowd. "Only the sophomores and the mighty seniors left! Who's it going to be?"

The seniors screamed and applauded, and Brett's grin disappeared.

Casey poked him in the ribs. "Guess they haven't heard that you were in charge yet."

Brett kicked at the frozen ground with his skate. "I wish he'd get on with it."

With great deliberation, the seniors were announced as the second-place winners. It took a minute for Brett to realize that meant that the sophomores won.

Casey gave his arm a victory squeeze. "You did it!"

"Yahoo," Brett grabbed Casey by the waist, lifted her into the air and spun her around.

Brett put her down to go forward and accept the trophy for the sophomore class. The senior president introduced him and told everyone about the exceptional polar bears, and urged the students to stop by and take a look.

Already red from the cold, Brett's cheeks flushed brighter with each compliment. Casey flashed him a victory sign and watched as he made his way back to her through a throng of kids who pounded him on the back and offered their congratulations.

"Now *you're* the star," Casey said as he finally reached her side.

"I can hardly believe it." He grabbed her hand. "Let's get out of this crowd."

"I knew you could do it," Casey said as they walked back on their skates toward the skating pond. She was extra careful not to wobble and twist an ankle.

When they reached the edge of the ice, Brett stopped and squeezed her hand. "Now all you have to do is win *your* championship."

"We're halfway to a full sweep. You've won your part tonight, and now it's my turn."

"Casey, I really want to wish you good luck. . . . Hey! I bet everybody's been saying the same thing."

"I'll need it all."

From his pocket, he pulled out an envelope and handed it to her.

Casey took it and felt something lumpy inside. As she began to rip open one end, Brett stopped her. "Don't open it! I want you to wait until you get to Oakland."

Raising an eyebrow, Casey gave him a quizzical look. "Any special time?"

"Just look at it before your first event. Maybe it will bring you extra luck. Not that you need it."

"I may need a lot. My beam will have to be absolutely perfect," Casey told him.

"Ha! I know you love that marvelous piece of torture."

"You get used to it," she said as she looked up at him.

"*You* may get used to it!" Brett paused, looking down at her. "Just remember—when you're out there competing—I'll be thinking about you," he said, kissing her on the tip of her nose.

That's all the luck I'll need, Casey thought as they walked onto the ice.

Chapter 13

★ ★ ★ ★ ★ ★ ★ ★ ★ ★

WITH Winter Carnival behind her, Casey worked hard to polish her routines for the rapidly approaching Elite Championships. Chip had been right about picking up the pace of her workout. But she didn't mind. She was reaching for her dream, and together, she and Jo had really pushed themselves.

With only two days remaining before they would leave, the two friends worked late Friday night on the balance beam.

Jo spun into a pirouette turn on the end of the beam and set up for her dismount. When she completed a double twist and landed solidly, Casey let out a long whistle.

"Way to go!" Enthusiastically, Casey punched Jo on the arm. "You're going to make Elite for sure."

"I don't know, Casey. Lately I've been wondering if I've really got the stuff," Jo admitted.

"Jo, you've never looked better!" Casey argued.

"But is that good enough? The competition is going to be fierce," Jo reminded her.

"Jo, while you were out in California, I was worried, too. I thought that staying here had made me lose my chance at the Olympics. Here you were, working with the great Krensky, and I was plodding along at Flyaway."

"Oh, Casey! And all the time I just wanted to be home with you and Monica. There was so much pressure out there, and . . . I sort of lost my confidence."

"You've been great since you came back. There's no reason you can't do it—if you believe in yourself." Casey knew she was starting to sound like her dad and Chip; but she agreed with their advice.

Jo swung onto the low bar. "It's scary when you reach the top. I got a taste of it in California, and I'm not sure I like it."

"We've got to do it for Chip, too."

Jo studied her friend's earnest expression. "You're right! I've got to stop wasting time on all these doubts. Chip's such a good coach. He's earned his chance to have some Elite gymnasts."

"Right on!" Casey shot her fist in the air. "Now let's see your diamond again."

The rest of the evening, things went well for the girls. Relieved that Jo seemed more relaxed, Casey was able to concentrate on her own routines.

Before she left, Chip called her into his office. "Excited?" he asked.

"Numb, I think. I can't believe it's all for real. It's been this far-off dream for so long, and now here it is!"

"That's a natural reaction. You may not believe any of it is actually happening until you get back." Chip sat down at his desk and put his feet up, while Casey dropped into the familiar stuffed chair. "Sometimes that feeling of awe puts off first-time competitors, but I think you can handle it."

Casey hoped so. Everyone said Chip was great at preparing his gymnasts mentally. She needed to be at her best to have a chance to make it. "I think I'm ready."

"No *think* about it. You need to be positive!" he urged her.

"Okay, I'm ready!" Casey shouted.

"That's my girl! I wanted to check on your vault. Are you sure you want to do the Yurchenko?"

"Of course." For months, Casey had been practicing the difficult vault, named after Natalia Yurchenko of the Soviet Union, who had introduced the move at the 1983 World Championships.

"Just checking. That vault's too dangerous if you aren't ready. I don't want to take any chance on your getting hurt."

"I really want to give this meet everything I've got. If I held back and then didn't make it, I'd be furious with myself for my whole life," Casey argued.

Chip swung his feet off the desk. "That's exactly what I wanted to hear. Now, go home and get some sleep. We still have a couple of days of polishing."

On her way home, Casey thought about the meet. She knew she really was ready for it. Her routines were perfect, including her beam combination and the Yurchenko vault. Now she just had to prove it to everyone else.

Casey pressed her nose against the van window as they drove down Lake Shore Avenue to the Oakland Auditorium. As they circled a lake in the middle of the city, she watched sunbathers stretched out on the grass, and several people feeding the ducks.

"Look! It says Lake Merritt!" Jo squealed over her shoulder. "I hope the hotel is nearby. Oh, look—there's a boat house!"

"We won't have much time for any of this," Casey reminded her friend, although she hoped they might squeeze in a few minutes to explore the area.

"I know," Jo said wistfully. "I'm just glad we're here. The plane trip was fun, but it's good to be back on the ground."

"I still can't believe I'm actually in California," Casey said as Chip pulled the van into a parking lot next to a huge building.

The girls climbed out, and Chip led them up the stone steps and then up to the balcony. Casey walked down the aisle to the front row and stood looking out over the empty auditorium. This was where they'd compete during the three days of the national qualifying meet.

As she stared at the huge floor, already covered with mats, it finally hit her. She was here. Her dream of a lifetime would soon begin, and the goal she'd worked so hard for was within her grasp.

It was only seventy-two points away.

If she could score that many points, she'd be an Elite gymnast. "I can do it!" she whispered to herself.

Footsteps echoed on the stairs behind as Jo joined her. "It's a big place, isn't it?" she said quietly.

"Chip said that Saturday night it will be full for the finals." Casey couldn't wait for the big event.

"Do you think we'll make the finals?" Jo asked.

Casey looked at her friend, whose eyes were wide with excitement. "They only take ten girls for each event for the finals, but the important time for us is Friday night after optionals. That's when they announce the Elites." Casey grabbed Jo's arm and gave it a squeeze. "This is it! What we've waited for the past ten years."

"Yeah, but now we have to prove ourselves." Jo shifted her weight from one foot to the other. "We're so close. But what if we're not good enough?"

"Then we'll come back next year with Monica. C'mon, Jo, you were always the most optimistic of all of us."

"I think I left some of that optimism at Krensky's in Southern California," Jo admitted shyly.

Casey squeezed Jo again. "Then I'll be optimistic for you. We're going to make it!"

"I hope you're right," Jo said, finally smiling.

Chapter 14

★★★★★★★★★★

CASEY stood waiting to march into the large auditorium for the optional section of the Elite meet and ran her hands over her leotard—one of the special ones Sarabeth had given her. She hoped it would bring her luck.

A nudge from Jo drew Casey's attention away from the crowds. Turning, she saw her friend shaking her hands, trying to get out some of the tension. "I'm scared," Jo said.

Casey nodded. "So am I. But we both did well last night in compulsories. We're going into this with good scores."

"I know, but I've got the jitters."

"Don't we all!"

A lively march was struck up, and the procession of gymnasts started into the auditorium, led by a younger girl carrying the International Gymnastics Federation banner.

Each gymnast stepped forward as she was introduced. Saluting the audience as her name was called, Casey shivered with goose bumps. There was no way to still the excitement. She'd finally reached the big time.

After two days of practice and the preceding night's compulsory competition, she and Jo were heading into the optional part of the meet. This night's scores, added to the previous night's compulsories, would determine whether they made Elite or not. Casey could feel the tension building with each minute.

After the introductions, they marched to their first event and sat down in the row of chairs for the floor exercise. Jo leaned over. "I wonder what Monica's thinking right now?"

"Probably that she's as good as anybody else here on floor ex." Casey stole a quick look at Monica; she was sitting with the Bensons, close to the front. Chip would have a fit, but she'd chance it. Monica saw her looking and gave her a thumbs-up sign.

"You never did tell me what Brett said in the letter he gave you," Jo remarked as the judges took their places on opposite sides of the spring floor.

"The envelope! I forgot it!" Casey pulled her duffel bag out from under her seat and retrieved the rather crumpled letter. With so much going on, she'd completely forgotten it.

She opened it and was surprised to find no note—only a bright yellow balloon on which he'd written, "Good Luck, Casey" with a thin Magic Marker.

Jo poked Casey. "What a sweetie! He even remembered the balloon."

Smiling, Casey tucked the balloon back into her bag. As wonderful as Brett was, she had to put him out of her mind. For the moment, she had more important things to do.

As the music for floor exercise started, Casey turned her attention to the girls in her rotation, as they performed unique routines choreographed to a wide variety of music. Watching all the different tumbling runs, she began to doubt her own skills.

She reached for Jo's hand, which felt clammy. Jo gave her a weak smile and whispered, "We can do it. That was *you* saying that, wasn't it?"

Casey nodded and grinned. Just the touch of her friend and the idea that they were in this together calmed her nerves, and she willed her pulse to slow down. So this was how it felt to be competing against the best.

Somehow, Casey and Jo got through their floor routines, and Casey relaxed. It hadn't been so bad after all. Now she could concentrate on the balance beam.

When Jo did her mount and began her routine, Casey followed each of her moves, amazed at the amount of confidence Jo had gained during her time at Krensky's. She might have been unhappy, Casey thought, but her gymnastics had reached a higher level. A needle split showed off her flexibility, and each of her leaps was high and effortless. Casey joined in the clapping when Jo finished her double twist dismount with no steps.

Now it was her own turn. Casey stood waiting

for her signal to begin. She visualized her routine, picturing each element as it led up to her layout combination. She'd soon see if all those hours—no, years—of practice would pay off.

The judge raised her little flag, and Casey mounted the beam. She pushed everything from her mind except the next minute and a half ahead of her. From a split, she pushed herself into a handstand and turned it in a circle, feeling her confidence build. Each movement flowed easily into the next, and when she approached the layout combination, she felt totally confident. Her back handsprings were solid, and she stretched out above the beam, for a second suspended in space. When she finished the combination, a smile burst onto her face, and she spun through her turn and dismounted with an extra spurt of energy.

After saluting the judge, Casey flew into Jo's arms. The applause from an enthusiastic audience rang through the auditorium. When the score flashed 9.8, an ecstatic Casey hugged her friend with vigor. "Jo! I did it! I really did it!"

"Of course, you did it. I knew you would!" Jo said as she hugged her friend." Hey, not so hard— I still have two events!"

Casey's group moved to the vault next, and every time a girl went over the horse, Casey thought that person's vault was better than the last one. "They're all so good," she whispered to Jo.

Jo rolled her eyes. "I was just looking for the nearest emergency exit," she joked.

"Maybe they'll be thinking the same thing about

us," Casey said as she got up. It was time to do her Yurchenko vault.

Chip carefully adjusted the springboard the way she liked it. It was important to line it up perfectly. On this vault, she would do a cartwheel, back handspring onto the springboard, launching herself backward onto the horse. Then she would spring off the other side in a tuck somersault.

As Chip stepped away from the board, the judge raised her flag to signal she was ready for the next gymnast. Casey stared down the runway at the horse. She'd have two tries, and the highest score would count, but she wanted them both to be good.

Taking a breath, she sprinted down the runway and launched herself into the vault. She took half a step on her landing, but she felt pleased, and Chip's grin threatened to split his face in half.

When Casey also nailed her second vault and sat down, Jo pounded her on the back and then got up to wait for the gymnast who was performing in between them to finish. Casey watched her friend step up to the starting position, looking very confident as she waited to see the score of the girl in front of her. Jo would also be doing a Yurchenko vault.

Heads bent together; the judges discussed the last girl's score. Casey decided this was one of the two worst moments in gymnastics—waiting to go on. The other was waiting to see your score.

Jo began to fidget when the delay lasted another minute.

"Don't let it get to you," Casey whispered under

her breath. She knew these few minutes would seem like a lifetime to Jo.

As if reading Casey's mind, Jo stepped away and went back to her stretches, as Chip had instructed them. He'd tried to prepare them mentally for every possible problem, and a delay in scoring was one of the most common. Jo finished stretching and shook out her ankles and rolled her shoulders, trying to keep loose.

Finally, satisfied with their decision, the previous gymnast's score flashed. Only a 9.2. Casey sighed with relief.

The judge signaled for Jo to begin. She ran hard and hurled herself into the roundoff. From her chair, Casey thought Jo looked a little off center as she came off the springboard.

In an instant, she knew Jo was in trouble.

Sucking in her breath, Casey gasped as her friend came out of the tuck somersault off to one side. Jo couldn't get both feet under her. She landed hard on one foot and staggered.

Casey jumped out of her chair as Jo crumpled to the mat.

Seconds later, Chip was at Jo's side examining her ankle. Horrified, Casey ran to them.

As Chip gently tested the foot, Jo grimaced in pain. Dropping to her knees, Casey took her friend's hand, and the other gymnasts who were at the vault crowded in behind them.

Casey wished they could stop the floor exercise. The lively, cheerful music was an unwelcome contrast to Jo's condition.

Jo tipped back her head and let out a long sigh. "Casey, I tried. Really, I did."

Casey patted her arm as Chip scooped Jo into his arms. "Get back, everybody!" he told the group. "Let's get her out of here!"

He carried Jo over to the side of the auditorium and settled her on the mat. Taking the bag of ice that a trainer offered, he applied it over the injured area that was already beginning to swell. Then he pulled her into a hug. "I'm sorry, babe."

"Am I really out, Chip?" Jo bit her lip in an attempt to stop the tears from coming.

"I'm afraid so. There's no way you can handle the dismount with that ankle." Chip looked at her leg and shook his head.

Casey stood next to them. She didn't know what to say. "Jo, you were so good tonight," she whispered.

Jo tried to smile, but instead, she began to cry. "I was going to make it, wasn't I?"

"You had it made. And now, all these people won't get a chance to see your awesome bar routine."

With tears in her eyes, Jo looked up at Casey. "Do it for both of us, Casey," she pleaded.

Casey gulped back tears of her own. Wiping one from her cheek, she realized she didn't have time for regrets or sadness right now—she had a big job ahead. Jo was the star on the bars at the Flyaway Gym Club, and Casey wondered if she could give an equal performance. She'd have to try harder than she ever had before on bars.

Casey moved to the last rotation—the one Jo had been counting on to win her a spot on the team.

When Casey stepped up to the uneven bars, she focused on the set of bars in front of her. The judges would be looking for a continuous, smooth flow of movement—and perfect precision—as she executed her difficult combinations. There wouldn't be room for even a slight hesitation or break in her routine.

With a fierce intensity, Casey mounted the bars and whirled through her series of complex swings and somersaults.

Seconds later, she knew she was giving the best performance of her life.

Casey felt only exhilaration as she swung into her reverse Hecht. On the high bar, she took a giant swing, almost to a handstand, before she dropped into a straddle. Releasing her hands, she soared over the bar, catching it again between her legs on the way down.

When she dismounted and held her position, she felt tremendous satisfaction. She'd done the best she could. And shortly afterward, a 9.85 proved her right.

Thrilled, Casey went over to sit next to Jo, and together they waited to hear who had made Elite. Ice packs covered Jo's ankle. Blinking back tears, she said, "Casey, you were great! I couldn't have beaten you tonight."

"That's ridiculous. You'd have blown me away if you hadn't gotten hurt."

Jo didn't bother to argue. She shifted her ankle and winced. Closing her eyes, she leaned back against the wall, content to hold Casey's hand while they waited.

The scores were tallied as suspense among the gymnasts intensified. The crowd began to stir, but few people left. Finally, the announcer called for quiet and began calling the names of the girls who'd qualified.

Casey held her breath as she waited while each name was called. What if she wasn't included? Her grip tightened on Jo's hand, and Jo squeezed back in support.

When Casey heard her own name, she screamed. Hugging Jo, she frantically searched the crowd for her parents and Monica. She saw her mother and father standing and applauding, and beside them, Monica was jumping up and down as though she were on a pogo stick. Casey thought she would burst with happiness. It had happened! She had made Elite.

As she headed for the floor, Chip grabbed her by the waist and whirled her around. "You're going to be number one someday!" he said.

When Chip set her down, Casey walked out onto the floor, feeling a mixture of exhilaration and sadness. She wished both Jo and Monica were walking with her. Jo's sprained ankle had pushed Casey to reach for perfection on bars.

And the push had paid off.

As Casey accepted her new rank of Elite, she knew it would bring many changes. Part of her life would go on hold. To become a world-class gymnast, she would need even more discipline, and she'd have time for little else except gymnastics.

But this was Casey's dream, and she reached out to take it.

Here's a look at what's ahead in ONE STEP AWAY, the fifth book in Fawcett's "Perfect Ten" series for GIRLS ONLY.

MONICA watched, fascinated, as the older boy came to life inside the circle of the sparkling light. Obviously Kyle Taylor was accustomed to being in the spotlight, and it brought out the actor in him.

"Now, sing your song, Kyle," Ross directed.

Kyle didn't hesitate for a moment. He began singing a fast-pace rock song right from the Top Forty charts. Monica thought he sounded *wonderful*. His voice was deep, and he sounded more like a grown man than a high school kid. It was also a powerful voice, carrying through the entire auditorium without the benefit of a microphone.

Monica watched as Kyle extended his arms in a professional way, even moving his body slowly, dramatically, the way a relaxed, experienced entertainer would. His smile as he sang was artificial, but somehow it was absolutely right for the lively song he was doing. Something about that smile made Monica catch her breath in sudden admiration. No doubt aobut it—Kyle Taylor knew how to captivate an audience.

"Now you keep dancing, Monica." While Monica started to dance, Kyle was instructed to go on singing his rock song. For a few minutes the music for each of their acts was playing at the same time. It sounded odd, though it was quite controlled.

But then slowly, at Ross's direction, the music stopped, and Ross explained that Kyle would begin singing a love song directly to Monica, as if he had fallen in love at first sight with the petite girl in the other spotlight.

"That's bizarre, Ross!" Ms. Mac cried. She sounded delighted.

"Of course it is," Ross said, proud of his idea. "We will be juxtaposing the singer with the classical dancer, and at intervals, they will look at each other."

"Wait," Ms. Mac said. "let me see if I'm getting this right. They're both auditioning, and they fall in love at the auditions. Is that right?"

"But of course! Don't you see?" Ross Hartley waved his arms around triumphantly. "It will be a love story! An unusual lvoe story that will unfold right on the stage, right during all the auditions that make up the acts."

"I love it," Ms Mac declared fervently.

"Sounds great!" Roxanne agreed.

"So the decision will be up to you two," Ross Hartley said. "Kyle? Monica?"

Kyle was looking at Monica with big, sincere eyes and she found herself staring back at him as if in a daze. Suddenly her heart flipped over inside her chest.

"How about it, kids? Would you be willing to work in a partnership like that?" Ms. Mac asked.

Monica saw Kyle nod eagerly, and she felt a shiver of delight.

"I'd love to do an act like that," Kyle said, speaking for the first time. "Monica would be a wonderful partner."

"Monica?" Ms. Mac pressed. "Would you be willing to break up your solo act this way? Would you work with Kyle?"

Monica was afraid she wouldn't be able to talk through the giant lump that was forming in her throat. Her pulse was racing double time. She hadn't even decided to be in the show, and yet they were all assuming she would be!

She felt she was standing at a gateway, and all she had to do was say the magic word and the gate would open. Inside was something she wanted very much: the thrill of the theater world, the admiration of audiences, and the excitement of working with Kyle Taylor.

But on the other side of the gate, pulling at her and telling her not to shortchange her gymnastics, were a host of people who were important: Monica's parents, Jo and Casey, Coach Bear Benson, Derek Stone, and of course, Chip Martin, her Flyaway coach . . .

"Well Monica? What do you think?" Ms. Mac pressed. "You'd be our AUDITIONS leading lady, in a way. Would you be willing to work with Kyle?"

Leading lady? Monica thougth in confusion.

Someone actually wanted her for a leading lady role, when Chip thought she wasn't good enough even to try out for Elite!

Monica nodded slowly. "Yes," she said. "I'll do it."